The Wild One

Published by Amorous Publishing

http://theodorataylor.com/

Copyright © 2012 Theodora Taylor

ISBN: # 978-1479289134

ALL RIGHTS RESERVED

WARNING: The unauthorized reproduction or distribution of this copyrighted work is illegal. No part of this book may be used or reproduced electronically or in print without written permission, except in the case of brief quotations embodied in reviews.
This is a work of fiction. All names, characters, and places are fictitious. Any resemblance to actual events, locales, organizations, or persons, living or dead, is entirely coincidental.

To my grandmother, who I would never let read this (whispers: because of all the s-e-x), but who taught me to love soap operas. Most of our favorite soaps are gone now, but they live on in my heart.

And to all my fellow soap opera fans, who I hope will enjoy this book most of all..

PROLOGUE

"**I'M** not sure I have this on right," Layla said on the other side of the bathroom door.

Andrew, who felt like he'd already been waiting a lifetime for Layla to come out, sat up on the suite's California king-sized bed. "How about you come out, and I'll let you know."

A moment later the door creaked open and Layla stepped out dressed in a peach bra that hardly covered the nipples of her dark chocolate breasts. The cups of the bra were tied together with a satin bow at the center of her chest, a bow that seemed to be begging Andrew to untie it and release the two bountiful treasures it was barely constraining. Underneath the bra, she wore a pair of matching peach panties, the crotch of which was sheer enough to frame the swollen lips beneath it.

White-hot bolts of lust shot through his cock, making him fully erect underneath his black briefs in an instant. "I'd say you have it on exactly right."

For a moment, Andrew held still, his mind in the throes of warring compulsions to strip her bare and savor the sight of her like this at the same time. Seconds ticked by and she seemed to grow even more nervous under his gaze, shifting from foot to foot next to his bed.

But Andrew kept her pinned with his eyes. He wanted her to fully understand the Andrew she remembered was no more. Her sweet and considerate college boyfriend was gone, replaced by an untamed animal who wanted nothing more than to devour her whole.

She wiggled her fingers at her side nervously. "So are

we going to…?"

He came across the bed in an instant, dragging her into his arms and covering her wide mouth under his with raw and naked hunger.

"Andrew," she moaned against his lips.

He forced himself to ignore the siren call of her breasts, and instead dug two fingers into her pussy. "Yes," he said when he found her wet. "I want you wet. I want you fucking dripping for me, sweetheart. I'm going to lie back, and I want to you ride me so hard I forget everything that went down between you and Nathan. Can you do that? Can you make me forget?"

She nodded and pushed against his fingers, so hot for him, she probably didn't even realize what she was doing.

Andrew had never come in his pants, even as a kid. But the sight of her writhing into the fingers he was thrusting in and out of her nearly undid him. He had to let her go or risk embarrassing himself.

And the last thing he wanted to do now that he had finally gotten Layla Matthews into his bed was come early.

He dragged his lips off hers and, even more reluctantly, removed his fingers from her hot pussy. As it was, he wasn't the least surprised when he took his cock out of his briefs and found it rigid, already dripping with pre-cum.

For a moment, an image of Layla sucking him off the night before with her sweet mouth invaded his mind. Even more pre-cum erupted from the eye of his dick. But that was last night. He had something else in mind for this afternoon.

He lay back on the bed. "Come on, sweetheart. Get on top."

Shy Layla was back now and once again, she didn't seem to know what to do with that luscious body of hers.

But Andrew was more than happy to tell her.

"Get rid of those panties, then crawl over to me on the bed and swing your leg over."

With tentative movements, she did as he asked, but before she could sit down on top of him, he said, "No wait a minute, stay kneeling. I want to look at you."

And look at her he did. Her naked cunt glistened, weeping with need in the soft afternoon light.

Finally he untied the bow, freeing her soft breasts to his hungry gaze.

"Invite me in," he said, his words thick with lust.

She once again hesitated, but then placed a finger on each lip of her pussy and pulled it apart wide for him, giving him the most blatant physical invitation a woman could give. His manhood pulsed in immediate answer, and his mouth began to water. Another fight erupted in his mind. He wanted to taste her so bad again, but he didn't think he could take not being inside her for even a minute more.

He wrapped his hands around her waist and pulled her down over his dick until he was buried deep inside of her.

She cried out. "Oh, Andrew!"

She was so fucking tight, like a velvet glove made just for him. If he had known they'd fit this well together, there would have been no way he'd let her stay with Nathan as long as she had. And for minutes on end, the only sound in the room was of their two hungry bodies slapping together.

But just as they were about to reach their apex, he stilled and stopped her hips from moving.

"Layla, tell me you want this," he said.

Layla seemed to be in a daze, wild with lust to the point that it took her several moments of trying without success to move her hips to realize he'd asked her a question.

But Andrew waited for her to figure it out. Considering how long he had waited for Layla, it wouldn't do to have his patience give out now, even if his cock was practically yelling, "Less talk, more rock!"

After the haze cleared from her eyes, she said. "I want this." Then she lifted her eyes to meet his. "I want you. The truth is, I've never felt like this before. I've never wanted anybody like this. It feels like my body is going crazy."

"You want this more than you want to be with Nathan?" Andrew should have felt like a heel for demanding her acquiescence this way, in the middle of sex. But when as much stuff had gone down between two people as it had between him and Layla, he couldn't blame himself for wanting to hear her say it. "Tell me you want me more than you want my brother."

"I want you more than I want your brother," she answered. No hesitation. No looking away. No way he couldn't see the truth of her words written across her eyes. "Andrew, I—I love you."

And despite all the nasty things he planned to do and say to her, his heart just about came apart with joy then. "It feels like I've been waiting my whole life to hear you say that. I love you, too, sweetheart. So fucking much."

He surged up into her, and soon, as if to prove the validity of her professed feelings, she was coming apart for him, clenching her teeth as the orgasm took her and then him in a tidal wave of desire.

Layla was his now. Fully his. She no longer wanted Nathan—she loved him. He had never been so happy in his life. He had finally landed the girl of his dreams.

And this time, he was not going to be a gentleman about it. God help both him and Nathan if his brother ever tried to get her back.

CHAPTER 1

Two weeks earlier...

MABEL scowled at Roxxy from behind the bright red, hydraulic barber chair. "You obviously hate me."

Roxxy plopped into the chair, which stood in the middle of what they referred to as "the closet," but what was really a repurposed, two thousand square foot room located off the master bedroom of her penthouse apartment. It had a view overlooking Central Park, and it was large enough to house her thousands of costumes, her extensive collection of wigs, and the special hair and makeup center where she'd met up with Mabel almost every single morning for the last several years.

"Good morning to you, too, Mabel," she said with a huge yawn.

"What have I told you about sleeping in your hair and makeup?" Mabel asked, snatching last night's powder-white, Marie Antoinette wig off her head. "You look like a raccoon prostitute. How am I supposed to get you ready for the *Today Show* looking this bad?"

Roxxy didn't bother to confirm Mabel's assessment of her looks in the mirror. She simply placed her chin into the palm of her left hand and let her head droop into it. "If I sit like this, can you still do your job?"

"You party too much," Mabel informed her. She pulled her own hair, which she wore in long dreadlocks, into a messy ball on top of her head and lodged them in place with a makeup brush.

"I know."

"I'm about this close to getting together with Dexter to stage an intervention."

Roxxy yawned again. "Doesn't announcing a plan for an intervention kind of defeat the purpose?"

"Keep joking, but I'm honest to God worried about you," Mabel said. She sprayed the short natural Roxxy wore under all her wigs with water, and rubbed a rich, moisturizing, leave-in conditioner into her tight curls. This routine was so familiar to Roxxy that it felt like both a massage and a ritual.

"I know you are," Roxxy mumbled, feeling a twinge of guilt for yet again making Mabel's life harder. "Maybe I'll check myself into rehab after my last show. *Or…*"

She let the "or" hang, knowing Mabel's busybody nature wouldn't let her not ask.

And she was right. "Or what?" Mabel snapped, dumping a copious amount of makeup remover onto a large cotton round.

"*Or*," Roxxy said, "You, Dexter, and me can take a vacation some place where the boys are as hot as the weather."

Mabel slapped her on the shoulder. "Dexter might like that, but what's an old lady like me going to do with boys your age?"

"You're only in your forties, Mabel," she reminded her. "And I'm thirty now. I think there are plenty of things you could do with a boy my age. You want me to spell it out for you?"

More often these days, Roxxy resented her role as one of America's sauciest, sexiest pop stars, but sometimes it was nice to let herself pretend she really was the kind of uninhibited woman who could actually seek out male attention without there being copious amounts of alcohol involved.

Mabel threw her head back with laughter. "You are *so* bad."

"Yeah, we're definitely going to go with the vacation option," Roxxy said, smiling as her eyes fluttered close. "I've been to rehab, and let me tell you...*boring*."

She started to drift off into blessed sleep—only to be jerked awake with a hard shake.

Even before opening her eyes, Roxxy knew it was Shirelle. Getting abruptly woken up by this woman was even more familiar than her multi-hour hair and makeup sessions with Mabel. Shirelle had been shaking her awake for one thing or another since the age of three, when they'd first come to New York to make it big.

Roxxy groaned in irritation, but Mabel nodded with approval toward Shirelle who was decked out in a yellow A-line dress, which showed off her shapely calves and ample chest. Despite the early hour, she wore a full-face of perfectly applied makeup topped off with a sleek ponytail that fell all the way down to her butt. "Hey, girl! Look at you working that yellow dress."

Roxxy knew for a fact Shirelle was almost fifty, but thanks to a few subtle procedures over the years and an almost maniacal commitment to staying fit, she could have easily passed for a woman even younger than Roxxy. In fact, very few people other than Mabel knew Shirelle wasn't just Roxxy's manager, but also her mother.

On the rare occasion that Shirelle and she where in a room together when Roxxy wasn't wearing a crap load of makeup and fake hair, she couldn't help but be taken aback by how much they looked alike. They had the same smoky brown skin, the same almond-shaped eyes, and even the same well-defined curves—though Roxxy's toned lines came from putting on hundreds of concerts over the course of her singing career instead of two-hour exercise sessions every morning like her mother.

"Look how great she looks first thing in the morning,"

Mabel said, wiping yesterday's stage make-up off Roxxy's face with vicious swipes. "And you look like you got punched in both eyes. Roxxy, why can't you be more like Shirelle?"

Shirelle preened under the compliment, but then glared at Roxxy. "And why aren't you practicing your vocal warm-ups for the *Today Show?*"

Roxxy threw her mother a sleepy smile, "Because I haven't had my morning tea yet."

On cue, Dexter, the bodyguard, who her team called the "Black Hulk" behind his back, appeared and placed a large cup of the special tea he ordered in bulk for her from an herbalist in his neighborhood.

"Thanks, Dex," she said. "Did you get one for yourself, too?" Never allowing herself to eat or drink alone had started out as a diet trick in her early twenties. But now it was so ingrained, it didn't feel like she would actually be able to consume anything without at least one other person in the room doing the same.

Dex produced his own thermos of coffee and took a sip, without speaking. As a rule, he didn't speak unless he absolutely had to. He seemed to consider talking about anything that didn't relate to Roxxy's protection or comfort to be a waste of time. Even now, his eyes were sweeping the room above his thermos for anything that could do his employer harm or cause her any discomfort.

These were just two of the many reasons why Dex was the only one other than Mabel and Shirelle allowed to see her without her stage makeup.

After a decade of only appearing in the most outrageous costumes and makeup, it had become the primary goal of a few photographers to capture a picture of her out of makeup. She liked most of the people on her team and trusted them with many of the most intimate details of her life. But she only trusted three people not to covertly take a picture of her real face and pass it on to a tabloid, blog, or paparazzo. And all three of those people were in this room. Even Roxxy's two assistants didn't get to see her out of makeup.

Dex yawned, trying to conceal it behind one beefy hand.

This immediately had Mabel clucking her tongue. "Poor baby. Did this one have you working security for her at them clubs all night again?"

Dexter didn't answer.

"You know, you can tell her no sometimes," Mabel said. "I'd never let her fire you."

Loyal as always, Dexter didn't answer. Instead he went back into the racks of costumes and started his morning perimeter sweep.

Mabel harrumphed. "Why that man is so dedicated to you, I don't know. If he really cared, he'd stop enabling you." Mabel turned to Shirelle, who was already steadily thumbing out business texts and emails as she did every morning. "Don't you think she should party less, Shirelle? Look how run down she is."

Shirelle barely glanced up from her smart phone. "I wouldn't mind if she got in front of the cameras more when she went out. The best scenario would be if she snagged a famous boyfriend. An actor would be nice, that way she'd get twice the coverage, and it would give her some star power when we move to California and start auditioning."

Just so she could get her mother off the subject of acting, a career move she had no intention of making, Roxxy launched into her morning runs.

A few hours and vocal warm-ups later, Mabel turned her around in the swivel chair, and she was once again,

Roxxy RoxX, the sexy, chart-topping, international music star who sold out stadiums and started cameras clicking whenever she entered a room.

Today Mabel had outfitted her in a humongous gray afro wig and a headband with triangular furry ears. These ears might have been mistaken for a cat's, if not for her face, which Mabel had made up to look like a raccoon's, with huge black circles around her eyes, highlighted by white makeup at her cheekbones, and gray makeup covering the rest of her face.

"Impressive, but you forgot the whiskers," Roxxy said, turning her face from side to side in the mirror.

"I'm sure people are gonna get what I'm going for." Mabel disappeared down one of the rows of costumes and reappeared with a slate gray mini-dress, which sported several tears in strategic places. "Especially after you put this on with a pair of black fishnets."

Her "raccoon prostitute" look was a big hit. The hosts of the *Today Show* crowed and chastised her appropriately, and she was already all over the gossip and celebrity sites by the time she hit the stage for the last concert of her world tour.

This one would be filmed and featured on HBO, so there were several costume changes and even a few retakes. Her whole team—especially Mabel—had to work like dogs to pull it off.

"I'm thinking of taking Mabel and Dexter on a vacation somewhere next week," Roxxy said as she, Dexter, and her mother drove home from Madison Square Garden in the back of a stretch limo.

"That's a great idea," her mother said. "Maybe we should all go to California. You could start meeting with film agents and a few acting coaches, so we can begin the next phase of your career."

"That's not exactly a vacation," Roxxy answered. "And I've told you like a million times already, I don't want to act."

Her mother gave her a concerned look. "Then what are you going to do with yourself? You're not going back into the studio until the fall, and the last time you had a break this long, I had to cut *my* vacation short in order to come back from St. Tropez and act as your monitor while you were under house arrest."

A small mine of regret went off in her chest. The first DUI she'd gotten had felt more like a rite of celebrity passage than a crime. She'd gotten pulled over soon after she'd left a club in the Hamptons. But then she'd gotten into another scuffle with the law less than a year later, and that hadn't been cute at all. Roxxy thanked her lucky stars that she had only totaled her car and hadn't actually hurt anyone in the accident that resulted in her DUI.

"I know you think I'm whining, but I really need a vacation. A real one. You have no idea how much." Roxxy said.

"Oh, I get it. You're nervous about meeting with agents because of your issues." Her mother pulled out a baggie of white pills. "You can take one of these. It'll calm your nerves, and if you really want to have a good time in California, just mix it with some alcohol, then you won't have to worry about being on if the agent invites you out to dinner later."

Roxxy gave her mother a withering look. "Do you want me to get another DUI?"

Her mother dismissed the question with a wave of her hand. "You're always coming back to that. It was just a little fender bender."

"They put me under house arrest!"

"You got a bad judge. He was trying to make an

example out of you because you're famous. Even your lawyers said so." Shirelle waved the bag of pills temptingly. "Give one of these a test drive tonight when you're out at the clubs. My connect says dancing on this stuff is amazing."

She thrust the bag toward Roxxy again, but Roxxy pushed it away. "You know, I don't mess with that stuff anymore. I don't need it."

"Well, obviously you do if it's keeping you from making our dreams come true in California."

A wave of tiredness washed over Roxxy and she rubbed her eyes. "Shirelle, just drop it. Please."

Her mother folded her arms and looked out the tinted window, letting her body language do the talking for her.

Roxxy had to bite the inside of her cheek to keep from apologizing. For quite a while there, she and her mother had actually been close, going out to clubs, taking extravagant vacations, and enjoying the perks of Roxxy's fame. But ever since the second DUI, their relationship had been strained. She could almost feel the disappointment coming off her sullen mother in the car. And heaven knew how Shirelle would react if she found out what Roxxy had really been doing with her nights or that she was planning to move to California, but not to pursue an acting career.

They spent the rest of the car ride in silence. Shirelle didn't even bother to say goodnight when she and Dex climbed out of the limo.

And if the argument with her mother hadn't made her feel bad enough, she once again had to ask Dex to go above and beyond the call of duty that night.

"It's two in the morning, Dex, and I hate to do this to you," she said. "But I'll probably be up all night again."

"It's okay," Dex said, shrugging. "How 'bout I hit two

clubs and call it quits in the morning?"

"And definitely don't bother to get here until I'm done with makeup. I've only got one last interview tomorrow on *The View*, then we're booking tickets to some place nice where I won't be pretending to party every night. I promise. I even invited Mabel along so she can think she's keeping me out of trouble."

A rare smile lifted the side of Dex's mouth. "She'll probably like that."

"Mother-henning me for a whole month on full salary? Oh no, you know she will *love it*. See you tomorrow."

Back to his usual silent self, Dex just nodded before opening the door for her. He did one last perimeter sweep of her entire apartment before he left. And even then he made sure the door was secure behind him.

Her heart swelled with appreciation as she listened to the familiar jangle of the door handle from the outside. She wished there was something more she could do for him other than give him a substantial bonus at the end of the summer. They had figured out that just his presence alone at a nightclub was enough to make people believe she'd been there whenever she needed to pull an all-nighter. And clubs being by their very nature greedy for any publicity they could get never refuted her presence when asked if it was true she'd spent all night on their dance floors. There had even been a few quotes from D-list celebrities, supposed "friends" of hers, who had "danced with her all night" and had seen her "locking lips" with a fellow celeb who just so happened to have a new movie or album out and needed the publicity.

Roxxy was so keyed up with adrenaline from her last show, she actually wouldn't have minded going to a club and dancing the night away, just like old times. But instead, she trudged up the winding stairs to the office loft where her laptop lived when she wasn't on the road. She tapped a key to turn it on, and it lit up on page five of the ten-page term paper final for her Sociology 101 class, which was due the next day. With grim determination, she started pecking out sentences, occasionally stopping to refer to the textbook, before going back to the keyboard.

This was the last paper of the semester and counted for a significant percent of her grade, so she couldn't just blow it off, no matter how exhausted she was. Also, these last few credits would complete her transfer requirements, making it possible for her to attend the University of Southern California as a full-time student. After that, she'd be on track to get a progressive bachelor's/master's degree in public administration, which would allow her to leave music behind forever and concentrate on her non-profit and philanthropic efforts.

She still hadn't figured out how to tell her mother that by this time next year, she'd have given up her career as Roxxy RoxX in order to attend school as simple Roxxanne Weathers. But she figured if she could handle taking classes while touring all over the world, she could handle telling Shirelle she was done with showbiz. Maybe. Possibly. She hoped.

On second thought, perhaps she'd just enroll and send Shirelle an email after she was firmly ensconced in her new apartment near the USC campus.

ROXXY WOKE UP THE NEXT MORNING, drooling all over her laptop keyboard. There were about fifteen pages of mumbo-jumbo from where various parts of her face had hit the keys. She'd have to ask one of her assistants to get her laptop cleaned since it was now covered in stage makeup. Again. But after deleting all the extra keystrokes, she found she was now only a paragraph or two away from finishing her paper.

Roxxy checked her smart phone. She had the appearance on *The View* this morning but she wouldn't be performing, just chatting with the show's hosts, so all she needed to do was get in hair and makeup. She grimaced, torn between making Mabel wait so she could type the last couple of paragraphs and getting to her makeup session on time.

In the end, she chose the term paper, figuring she'd be a better interview if she didn't have the final hanging over her head. Fifteen minutes later, she uploaded her work to her online classroom, then ran down the stairs and through the closet's door, calling out, "Sorry, I'm late! Really sorry!"

However, she found Mabel sprawled out in the makeup chair with her back to her. Apparently, she was so tired from yesterday's insane list of events, she'd fallen asleep waiting for her only client, who was late. Again.

A none-too-small pang of guilt hit Roxxy. She was aware by not going through the simple step of removing her makeup the night before—the only thing Mabel ever asked of her, really—she made her hair and makeup routine that much longer for her friend. Not to mention she was only a few months away from letting the woman go for good.

Roxxy vowed to do better during the rest of their time together and find Mabel another gig before she started college.

But meanwhile, she couldn't resist joking with the older woman, who she'd never caught sleeping on the job before.

"Hey, I thought I was the one who was supposed to come in here and fall asleep in the chair. You're stealing

The Wild One

my thunder." Roxxy whipped the chair around playfully.

But Mabel wasn't sleeping. In fact, her eyes were wide open and there were thin streams of dried blood trickling from her mouth and nose, like a terrible Halloween special effect Mabel might have dreamt up for Roxxy.

Mabel's new look had nothing to do with Halloween, though. Roxxy knew this because it was July. And also because of the note she found written on the mirror in the same black makeup Mabel had used to achieve the raccoon prostitute look the day before.

It read, "A GIFT TO YOU FROM ME. LOVE, YOUR BIGGEST FAN."

That's when Roxxy screamed and screamed and screamed some more.

CHAPTER 2

THIS would be the case that made his career. Even as Steve Kass handed a tissue to the woman crying in his guest chair, he could think of little else. If he managed to not only keep Roxxy RoxX alive, but also catch her murderous stalker, goodbye assistant D.A., hello Attorney General of New York come the next election cycle. Maybe Roxxy would even sing at his inauguration. How cool would that be? A chart-topping music star, playing at *his* inauguration? He could almost see it now...

"I'm sorry I'm crying all over your chair, Mr. Kass," Roxxy said, interrupting his inauguration daydream. "I just can't believe Mabel's really gone. She's been with me since I was sixteen. She was like a mother to me."

Her face, which was painted white with a rainbow of lightning bolts across it, crumpled as more tears fell from her eyes.

Steve held out another tissue. "No, don't apologize. You've been through a lot today between finding your employee like that and the hours of police questioning. I'm surprised your makeup held up all this time."

Roxxy, he noticed, hesitated a bit, before she plucked the proffered tissue from his hand, careful to avoid skin-to-skin contact. She'd also hesitated before shaking his hand earlier. He would have chalked it up to her being one of those germaphobe types, but she hadn't availed herself of the hand sanitizer on his desk after he invited her to sit down. And she was still calling him Mr. Kass, though he'd told her she could call him Steve twice already. There'd also been the loud way her behemoth of a bodyguard had announced he'd be right outside the door earlier, as if he were both assuring Roxxy and warning Steve.

Overall, the real life version of Roxxy RoxX was a lot less sassy and confident than the girl he'd seen in the music videos, first as a jailbait teen at the beginning of her career, and then as a naughty seductress with an even naughtier singing voice.

She sniffed behind her tissue. "Mabel was very good at her job. She always said if she was doing my makeup, it wouldn't come off until I wanted it off."

He eyed her get-up from the powder-blue mermaid wig that fell all the way down to her lush breasts, to the sequined green mini skirt that barely covered her ass, much less her shapely legs, which were encased in glittery tights. "You know, your penchant for makeup might serve us well when it comes to protecting you."

"How so?"

"Well, obviously, this is the work of an unstable fan. Luckily your bodyguard provided us with a list of people who have sent you unsettling emails and/or letters. However, it's really long."

Roxxy dabbed at her eyes. "That's why he never lets me check my own fan mail...he wants to keep me away from stuff like that."

"I don't blame him. But unfortunately, it's going to take a while for the NYPD to get through the list. Meanwhile, I think it would be best if you lay low, no makeup, no costumes, no—" he waved a hand toward the crazy wig, "—hair, except for your own."

Roxxy thought about that and nodded. "I was planning to take a vacation anyway. I could go to my condo in Atlanta. Or my flat in London. I'm also about to close on a new apartment in L.A. I could stay there."

"Actually, I was thinking someplace even less conspicuous than that. This guy broke into your high-security apartment and kept his face off all the cameras. I don't think going to another known residence is the answer. I also don't think you should stay with anyone you know, especially if they're also famous. In celebrity cases like yours, it's hard to keep locations contained. People want to give you safe harbor, but they also can't resist telling a friend or two that they've got a music star staying with them."

"I could stay with my bodyguard. He lives in the Bronx. I doubt anyone would look for me there."

Steve shook his head. He'd had a hard enough time convincing the large man to remain outside the door while he had this private conversation with Roxxy. He could only imagine how hard he'd make Steve's life if she were staying in his home.

"Unfortunately, Dexter isn't the kind of guy who blends in. And from what you've told us, the public has become used to associating him with you. Half of today's gossip blogs are reporting you spent the night at two different clubs and then found Mabel dead, just because he was spotted at both places."

She lowered her tissue. "So you want me to stay with a stranger?"

"It wouldn't exactly be staying with a stranger. I have a friend named Andrew Sinclair from college who owns a really nice guest ranch in Montana. I use him whenever I need a place to stash VIPs—usually people who witnessed big crimes.

"I didn't tell him who you were, but he's agreed to give you one of his cabins for as long as you need it. I think between hiding you out in a flyover state, keeping your identity a secret even from him, and the fact so few people have ever seen you outside of your stage persona, we should be able to keep you hidden until we flush out your stalker."

He half-expected her to fight him on this. Heaven knew most of the high-profile stalking victims who came through here seemed more concerned with keeping their careers on track than protecting themselves against possible psychos.

But Roxxy agreed with a quick nod of her head. "I'll go. I'll stay low wherever you want me to and however long you need. Only one thing," She gave him a sheepish look. "Could you tell Dex for me? I don't think he's going to take it well."

ROXXY WAS RIGHT, Dexter didn't take it well. After Mr. Kass told him, he all but pushed the smaller man aside to confront Roxxy.

"How could you agree to this?" he asked. "We don't know this guy. And how are you going keep yourself from freaking out when you're alone with him if I'm not on the other side of that door?"

"He's a civil servant. I'll just concentrate on that and I'll probably be fine."

Dex clenched his jaw, "Probably isn't good enough."

She rubbed his shoulder. "I know, Dex. But think of it as a trial run for when I go to college, okay? I mean, I'm going to have to learn to get along without you, anyway. Might as well start now."

"Can you call me when you get wherever he's taking you?"

She tilted her head to the side in apology. "I don't think so. I trust you, but he's not even letting me tell the guy I'm staying with who I really am. He also had me hand over my phone and wallet, so that I can't be tracked down. But I promise to be in contact as soon as I get back."

Dexter let his ham-like fist curl and uncurl in

frustration before finally saying, "Fine, I just worry about you all the time. You know that."

"I do." She hugged Dexter. He was the only man she'd felt comfortable enough to embrace in almost fifteen years, not just because he wasn't into girls that way, but also because he'd been so kind about putting up with all of her issues over the years. "I'm going miss you," she said, meaning it.

"Imma miss you, too," he said, hugging her back.

"You should do something for yourself while I'm gone," she told him. "Maybe take a vacation, like we were talking about before. You totally deserve one."

Dexter gave a non-committal grunt before saying, "Let me go give this fool some instructions before you leave."

She watched him walk away, back toward Mr. Kass. *You can do this, you can do this*, she chanted to herself, and she almost believed it.

CHAPTER 3

***SHE** couldn't do this*, Roxxy thought to herself an hour later. She and Steve Kass were on a private plane headed to Montana, and the only thing keeping her from having a full out panic attack in an enclosed space with a man she barely knew, was the bottle of vodka she was currently white knuckling between much needed swigs of Dutch courage.

She silently thanked her mother for shoving the vodka into her purse when she'd come to say goodbye to her at Mr. Kass's office. At the time, it had felt like her Shirelle being pushy again, but now the vodka was the only thing keeping her from jumping out of her skin.

And it was certainly the only thing allowing her to pretend she was a normal woman who could sit across from a man without her bodyguard nearby and without feeling completely creeped out.

"He's a civil servant. He's a civil servant," she chanted in her mind. Then she forced herself to listen to what Steve Kass was saying.

"After you take your makeup off, we'll go over the cover story we're going to give my friend, Andrew, and the second cover story we're going to give anyone else you meet. The most important thing for you to remember is you've got to stick to both stories. Andrew's a stand-up guy, and I trust him more than I trust most, but you never know how people will respond to star power, so you've got to memorize both your cover stories and stick to them no matter what, okay?"

"Okay," Roxxy agreed, taking another swig of vodka.

"Your manager, Shirelle, said you were interested in breaking into acting next, so this might come in handy for you."

Roxxy resisted the urge to roll her eyes. She'd have to be knee-deep in her degree before Shirelle gave up that dream.

"Anything else I should know before we get there?" she asked.

"Before I forget." He pulled a business card out of his wallet and placed it on the table in front of her. "If we get separated for any reason, or something important comes up and you can't get a hold of me, here's the D.A.'s number. He's the only other person I trust in my office not to leak your whereabouts."

"Okay," she said again, picking up the card and slipping it into her purse. "By the way, how am I supposed to buy anything if I don't have my credit cards?"

"I'll give you cash before we meet with Andrew. He'll need to take you to buy some new clothes tomorrow morning anyway, since you'll stand out too much in that outfit. But the guest ranch is all-inclusive, so you probably won't need much in the way of money. If you do want to buy something at the ranch, just charge it to the room. "

Ugh, going shopping the next day meant spending even more time alone with another man she didn't know. Roxxy had to take another swig of vodka to digest that information.

A few hours later, she found herself ensconced inside a bathroom at the Ride 'Em Cowboy, a two-floor motel with a diner attached. The motel appeared to be the only non-agriculture based business for miles and miles and it rented rooms by both the week and the night. Mr. Kass apologized profusely for putting her up there, but it was the closest hotel to Andrew's guest ranch, and it allowed him to pay for a week up-front in cash, so he wouldn't have to worry about anyone tracing his credit card to track

The Wild One

her down.

She'd already been inside the bathroom for at least twenty minutes, staring into the mirror over the sink. Though she'd sworn off drinking alone—especially if it was alcohol after her second DUI—she was already halfway through the bottle of vodka. Her hands shook as she unscrewed the lid of her makeup remover.

Roxxy had always thought when she finally took off the crazy makeup and the wild wigs and the outrageous costumes, it would be for something big: an exclusive with a popular talk show host or the final number at her last concert or the inevitable "Where are They Now" special ten or twenty years after her unofficial retirement.

But her final concert had come and gone unannounced because she was too chicken to tell her mother she was done with music, and where she was *now* was in a motel bathroom. With a half-empty bottle of vodka.

""How much longer?" the assistant D.A. called through the door.

A cold shiver crawled down her back. The only thing scarier than being alone in close quarters with a guy without Dex nearby, was taking off her makeup so she could do it again in a seedy motel room. It felt like the equivalent of a soldier throwing away her shield just before she was about to engage in battle.

"We're set to meet Andrew in less than thirty minutes," Mr. Kass said, reminding her he was still outside the door and waiting for her to answer.

Roxxy took several more swigs of vodka. "I'm going to need at least twenty more minutes," she called back.

Suddenly the room was no longer staying put the way it was supposed to. She turned away from the mirror just for a second or two, she assured herself, to give herself some breathing room. Looking around the bathroom, she took in the bathtub, solidly rectangular with a plastic shower curtain and no extra amenities like a Jacuzzi option or an array of expensive bath oils awaiting her on its ledge. There wasn't even a bar of soap that she could see.

What really struck Roxxy, though, was the smell. Or rather the lack of smell—no Jasmine or other aromatic scent being pumped through the circulation system. No cleaning products still lingering in the air, giving away that the room had received an extra special cleaning in preparation for her celebrity arrival.

The toilet was a dull white and so was the sink, which was encased in scratched-up, mustard yellow formica, probably dating back to the sixties or seventies. Nothing in the room sparkled underneath the fluorescent lights. In fact, they made her look garish and silly in the mermaid outfit, which had looked so magical the night before.

Finally the room stopped spinning, and the vodka must have really decided to kick in, because Roxxy didn't feel so scared anymore.

She turned back to the mirror and before she could think too hard about it, she poured a liberal amount of makeup remover onto a large cotton round. Then for the first time in over a decade, she began removing her makeup herself, with hard, determined swipes.

IT WASN'T LIKE STEVE WAS ONE OF THOSE HOUSEWIVES who read glossy magazines, lapping up news about the latest Roxxy RoxX exploits while clucking her tongue. However, he wasn't unaware of her reputation for partying hard and kicking up a tornado's worth of behind-the-scenes drama. That morning, in fact, he'd read all about her two DUIs and subsequent house arrest.

But he also knew she had millions of fans, and the truth

was, he'd heard quite a few of her throaty bubblegum songs on the radio and he hadn't always switched the station when he did. Sometimes he'd even found himself singing along. She had a really good voice, and they wrote those damn songs to stick in your head, even when you didn't want them to.

But standing in the motel room, waiting for her to emerge from the bathroom, he couldn't shake the nervous energy popping around inside of him. He, Steve Kass, would soon be the first regular person to see Roxxy RoxX outside of her elaborate hair and makeup in over a decade. If everything went to plan, and she was able to lay low at Andrew Sinclair's ranch until they tracked down her stalker, maybe he'd be the only person to knowingly see her this way.

He was so nervous, he decided to busy himself with making her a cup of her special tea. Her monolith of a bodyguard, Dexter, had given it to him right before they left the station, with the instructions that Roxxy hated eating or drinking any beverage alone, so he had to drink it with her. Like a lot of people who worked for celebrities, the guy seemed to think his employer's every peccadillo was sacrosanct and therefore should be accommodated by anyone who came in contact with her. Also, he'd noticed Little Miss Rockstar didn't seem to have any problems guzzling vodka down on the plane.

But in this case, Steve didn't mind indulging Dexter's order. It gave him something to do with his hands. Maybe he and Roxxy could have a cup of it together after she came out, and that way he'd be able to cover up his nervousness about seeing the real her.

But the tea took less time to make than he thought it would. And soon it began to grow cold.

"How much longer?" he called through the door, now

more worried about giving one of the biggest music stars in the world ice-cold tea.

No answer, but he was fairly sure he heard the distinct sound of a bottle clinking against the sink. Was she still drinking in there? He guessed the gossip blogs hadn't been exaggerating about her party girl ways.

"We're set to meet my friend in less than thirty minutes."

"I'm going to need at least twenty more minutes," she called back. Her words were slurred, which made Steve wonder if she was drinking because of her current stalker situation or because she was about to walk out of the room, looking like a regular person, for the first time in almost fifteen years.

Probably a combination of both, he thought twenty minutes later, after knocking back both cups of now-tepid tea, before refilling them with bottled water, and setting both to warm in the microwave.

He was just taking out two new packages of the special tea, when the first pain hit him. It felt like a thin flash of lightning slicing across his chest. But that was nothing compared to the second bolt of pain, which felt like nothing less than an iron hand squeezing his heart to the point that he couldn't breathe. Something hot and sticky began to leak from his mouth as he banged a fist against his chest, trying to unhinge whatever had gotten a hold of his heart.

And for a moment it worked. The pain suddenly stopped, allowing him to breathe normally again.

"Mr. Kass?" a tentative voice came from behind him.

He turned around, and then once again reeled, this time with confusion. Because Layla Matthews, Andrew Sinclair's ex-girlfriend, was standing in the doorway of the bathroom.

"Layla, what are you doing here?" he asked. "Where's Roxxy?"

"What?" she said. She stepped toward him. "Are you hurt? You've got blood coming out of your mouth."

But before he could answer, a third pain exploded in his chest, this one more powerful than the first two combined. It blinded him and put him on his back.

I've been poisoned, he suddenly realized, his mind flashing to Roxxy's overly protective bodyguard. He opened his mouth to tell Layla what he had just realized, and who had given him the tea, which had obviously been meant to kill both him and Roxxy. But he choked on the blood running down his throat and spilling from his mouth. All he could do was cough and gaze upon Layla with helpless, mute frustration.

It had been over a decade since he'd seen her last, but she was still so pretty with her short curls and impossibly large brown eyes. She looked like an angel, her head haloed in the motel's fluorescent light.

For a moment he wondered if she was a hallucination, a by-product of whatever was working its way through his system. Or maybe this was what happened when you died. You got a vision of one of the nicest and cutest people you'd ever met to guide you home. If that were the case, then maybe dying wouldn't be so bad.

Still, his last thought was to regret he would not be able to one day brag to his colleagues about seeing Roxxy RoxX in real life. Because his own real life was over.

CHAPTER 4

FIRST she was downing the last half of a bottle of vodka in a motel bathroom, and then she was watching the man that had been in charge of escorting her to safety coughing up what looked like buckets of bloods before dying on the motel room floor.

This time she didn't scream. Instead the room closed in on her, growing hot as a furnace and spinning to the point that her body compelled her through the door and out into the fresh air, lest she throw up all over the assistant District Attorney's body.

It took several huge gasps of air before the urge to expel the small meal she'd had on the plane and the copious amount of vodka from her stomach passed. And even then, she only just managed to stagger to her feet, the world still swaying around her.

Unfortunately, not even the gruesome scene in the motel room was enough to sober her up after all the vodka she'd consumed, but she had to get Mr. Kass some help.

"Need pay phone," she slurred to herself, stumbling toward the diner portion of the motel.

On her way into the room, she had noted the presence of an ancient, glass pay phone box between the motel and diner. She now started toward it, determined to call 9-1-1 and get someone to help poor Mr. Kass no matter how inebriated she was, even if the short walk to the pay phone felt like trudging through mud. The stilettos she was wearing were like sandbags attached to her feet, and her large designer handbag, which had somehow stayed on her arm through the whole ordeal, felt like one of the jumbo kettle bell weights her mother swore by for workouts.

She was halfway to the glass-enclosed box when

The Wild One

someone behind her said, "Layla?"

What was with people calling her Layla? Mr. Kass had done it, too. But her name wasn't Layla, so she ignored whoever it was.

But the man's voice came again, this time closer and much louder. "Layla!"

Her plan was to keep on walking, no matter how much the night was swaying around her, but whoever it was grabbed her arm and turned her toward him.

She blinked, then blinked again. Standing before her in a cowboy hat and business suit, with his shirt collar open at the front, was maybe the hottest non-celebrity man she had ever laid eyes on. Long, lean, and clean-shaven with gray eyes, he'd give any number of the male celebrities she'd encountered a run for their money with a face that looked like it had been sculpted to please, from his long nose to his sharp cheek bones.

He stared back as if the sight of her had stunned him just as much as it did her. "Layla," he said again. "What are you doing here? Where's Nathan?"

She was about to tell him she wasn't Layla and she had no idea who Nathan was, but could he please help her call 9-1-1 because, weird story, her stalker had obviously followed her to Middle of Nowhere, Montana, and now the assistant District Attorney of New York was lying dead in a nearby motel room.

But she didn't have a chance to say any of this, because without warning, everything she had eaten that day and what tasted like the entire bottle of vodka came roaring out of her stomach, and yes, she threw up all over the hot guy's hand-tooled cowboy boots.

"Sorry," she managed to croak out right before she pitched forward and blackness enveloped her.

WHERE SHE LANDED WAS IN ANDREW SINCLAIR'S ARMS.

"What the hell?" he said, then immediately felt bad for cursing, because this was Layla, and he had always felt bad using explicit language in front of her. The only other time he'd ever really done it was when she announced, with tears in her eyes that she was breaking up with him because she was in love with his brother.

But then again, the Layla he knew would never show up in Montana unannounced, wearing what looked like a sequined mini skirt straight out of a music video and reeking of alcohol. He'd never seen her drink more than a glass or two of wine, much less enough alcohol to make her pass out. What was going on? And why was she here?

He pushed his many questions aside and shifted her so she was cradled in his arms. Then he bent down and picked up her large purse, which had slid off her arm when she fainted. Luckily the motel/diner, which didn't see much of a clientele on weekdays—its local nickname was the "Food Poison 'em Cowboy"—was particularly dead on this Monday night. So he didn't have to deal with nosy townspeople asking him why he was carrying an unconscious black woman back to his vintage '57 Chevy pickup.

Seeing as how he had just bought the entire ranch town of Frasier, Montana and renamed it Sinclair Township, this was not the kind of attention he wanted from the townspeople or its few visitors.

But he was less worried about that, and more about the woman in his arms. There was one other car in the parking lot, a rental, which he recognized as the same non-descript, mid-sized economy car Steve always drove when he dropped off his "guests." He assumed Layla must have bussed into town, since the diner also served as a drop-off point for the Greyhound. But why would she take the bus as opposed to flying into Missoula and driving in?

After depositing her into the passenger side of his truck and cleaning off his boots the best he could, Andrew got out his cell phone to call his old roommate who he was supposed to meeting for a "highly sensitive drop off," which Andrew assumed was code for yet another mob informant—someone Steve needed him to hide in one of his guest cabins until he was called to the stand to testify.

The truth was, Andrew had less than zero time these days. He was in the midst of converting Sinclair Township into America's largest chain of guest ranches. But Steve was an old buddy, and even though he'd managed to disconnect from most of the people he used to hob-knob with back when he'd been an executive for his family's steel company, he somehow couldn't shake the slick roommate from New Jersey who'd grown up to be an even slicker assistant D.A. in New York.

However, now he had to let his old friend down or at least be late, both of which Andrew hated to do. But what was he going to do? Leave Layla passed out in his truck, while he went in and got some former mobster from the diner?

"Hey, Steve," he said, after the voicemail message finished. "Something came up and I need to meet with you later, maybe tomorrow morning. Call me back and we'll set up a time."

He re-pocketed his smartphone inside his suit jacket and looked over at Layla slumped down in the front seat. Steve hideout request wasn't the only thing he didn't have time for.

Even passed out, she looked more beautiful than ever. She'd lost what had to be at least fifteen pounds, but not in a bad way. She'd clearly been working out. And her skin glowed in the moonlight, looking just as dewy and fresh as it had back in college. With her hair also cropped short, like she'd worn it in college, it was hard to believe she'd aged a good twelve years since they'd dated.

Was it the Montana air? Because he hadn't remembered her looking this good the last time he'd seen her at her wedding to his brother. Back then, he'd conceded her to Nathan like a gentleman. And he'd left Pittsburgh determined to think of her as a sister as opposed to his ex-girlfriend.

But the way his dick rose in his pants despite the vomit he'd had to wipe off his boots told him he had clearly not succeeded in putting her in the friend zone. Before his mind could go any further with thoughts of what was under that ridiculous mini skirt of hers, he once again pulled out his phone and called his brother.

It went straight to voicemail. "Guess what? I'm on vacation and not coming back until August. If it's important, leave a message and my assistant will get back to you. Otherwise, give me a ring when I'm back in town."

"Hey, it's your brother," Andrew said after the beep. "Call me back when you get this. I think you know why."

He hung up and frowned at Layla's prone body. The last time Nathan had left Layla alone and gone on vacation like this, they'd fallen out, due to a misunderstanding. As in love with Layla as Nathan had claimed to be back when Andrew saw them last, this could only mean one thing: they had broken up.

Again, Andrew's dick jumped in his pants, this time demanding he take back what his brother had stolen.

But things had changed since the last time he and Layla saw each other, he reminded himself. Changed for the better. He had new life now, a better one, and had finally managed to shake free of his past.

And there was no way he was going to allow anyone, even someone he used to love as much as Layla Matthews, ruin that.

CHAPTER 5

ROXXY awoke to a feeling that used to be familiar, but that she hadn't had ever since she swore off hard partying and vowed to get her act together. That was right after she spent a few months with an alcohol-monitoring bracelet around her ankle, taking court-mandated breathalyzer tests until she'd proved she was truly on the wagon. Many of her friends from back then had gone through the same thing, and went right back to partying after the bracelet was removed. But the whole situation had embarrassed and humiliated Roxxy to no end.

She spent a long time after castigating herself and thinking about what could have happened if she'd run into another car as opposed to a telephone pole. No, she'd decided then and there she didn't want to spend her life in and out of rehab. She was better than that, or at least she knew she could be.

So why then was she waking up beneath cool white sheets in a strange bed and with a massive hangover? She sat up slowly, so as not to exacerbate the elephant popping and locking inside her head, and that's when it started coming back to her.

Finding Mabel's body the morning before, flying out to Montana, deciding to use a little Dutch courage to get through taking off her makeup for the first time in over a decade. And then...nothing. What happened after that?

"You're awake," a male voice said.

She nearly jumped out of her skin when she saw a very tall and ridiculously handsome man sitting in a wooden chair near the foot of her bed. (Or was it his bed?)

She'd slept with someone, too? She couldn't believe it. Roxxy hadn't slept with anyone in years. Literally years.

In fact it'd been so long, she was almost certain she had cobwebs down there. Dealing with her neuroses when it came to intimacy had been frustrating, to say the least. It used to be alcohol and occasionally a hard drug had been the only things that helped her calm down enough to hook up with a guy, which meant when she swore those off, she'd pretty much committed herself to a life of celibacy.

"I can't believe we slept together and I don't remember it! You're so cute. What a tragedy," she said, then slapped a hand over her mouth, realizing she'd spoken out loud. There must have still been some alcohol in her system. Usually when Roxxy woke up with a guy she didn't know, all she cared about was getting as far away as possible, as quickly as possible. But this was…different.

Tall and Handsome gave her a quizzical look. "We didn't sleep together. You passed out and I brought you back here."

Oh. She looked around. "Here" was a room with a large bed, a stone fireplace, and pale yellow walls adorned with framed photos of horses running across what she assumed were Montana landscapes. The surroundings were completely foreign to her, yet perfectly cozy.

"Sorry for passing out," she said. "I'm assuming I did some equally embarrassing stuff before that."

He got up, poured her a glass of water from a metal pitcher sitting on the rustic wood nightstand beside the bed, and handed it to her. "Well, only if you consider throwing up on my favorite pair of boots embarrassing."

She did. She most definitely considered that embarrassing. "Sorry about the throwing up part, too." She took several large gulps of water.

He sat back down but didn't say anything, just watched her drink. She didn't feel the usual panic set in, but she began to become uncomfortable beneath his steady gaze.

To the point that she immediately refilled her glass as soon as the first one was finished, just so she'd have something to do that didn't involve embarrassing herself any further with words.

"What are you doing here, Layla?" he asked before she had a chance to refill the glass a third time. Apparently, he had caught on to her delay tactic.

Why did he keep calling her "Layla?" Had she given him a fake name last night? Then she remembered what Mr. Kass had said on the plane, about sticking to her cover story no matter what. Was this the name she was supposed to be going by?

"So, I'm Layla. And this is one of your guest cabins?" she said. "You're the guy I came here to meet?"

Again with that quizzical look. "Not exactly. This is a bedroom in my house, which, yes, is a duplicate of the other houses on the ranch. Since it's prime vacation season, none of the other houses or cabins are available right now. And yes, I'm assuming I'm the guy you came out to meet, or else why would you be in Montana?"

That should have cleared it up, but his answer only confused her more. "Listen, obviously I was not at my best last night. Can we just go over my cover story one more time?"

He frowned. "You want a cover story?"

She put down her glass on the nightstand. "I'm assuming that's what we discussed last night, right?"

He shook his head. "Actually, we didn't really discuss anything last night. I found you wandering around drunk in the parking lot, and then you threw up and passed out."

"My sexiest performance yet," she couldn't resist joking, though she was aware he wouldn't get it since he don't know who she really was. "So we just met? You don't know anything about…"

She stopped herself, remembering at the last minute how Mr. Kass had expressly warned against telling anybody, even this Andrew guy, that she was a rock star who was currently trying to stay low until her stalker was found.

Andrew crossed his arms. "No, I don't know anything about what happened between you and Nathan or why you're here. But you don't need a cover story. You know my policy on honesty. We'll stick to the truth. You're my sister-in-law and you're visiting me."

She looked at him, confused. "But I'm not your sister-in-law."

He sat forward, a series of emotions darting across his face. "So it's true. You and Nathan have divorced, and it's official."

She was now wildly confused and had no idea how to answer this. "Um..."

"Okay, you don't want to talk about Nathan. Then do you want to talk about why you decided to come to me, as opposed to one of your girlfriends?"

And that's when she began to understand. "Layla" wasn't her cover story, she was somebody real, and this guy thought Roxxy and Layla were one and the same.

Roxxy resisted the sudden urge to roll her eyes. She had nothing against white guys, especially ones who looked as good as this one, but she'd lost count of how many times she'd been mistaken for her closest rival, a rapper-cum-singer who also dressed in outrageous outfits and probably wouldn't be recognizable without makeup or her infamous butt (which was rumored to be prosthetic), even though they had totally different body shapes and Roxxy was about ten shades darker.

Some white people just couldn't distinguish between black women, and apparently this guy had mistaken her for his sister-in-law, who she assumed was the only other black woman he knew.

Roxxy was just about to open her mouth to inform him she wasn't who he thought she was when quite suddenly, talking no longer became an option. One moment the guy was in his chair, the next he was beside her on the bed, pulling her into his arms and covering her mouth with his.

And boyo, this guy might not be able to tell the difference between black women, but he kissed as good as he looked. Everything in her body lit up like a Christmas tree and it felt like the nerves leading directly to her sex were waking up from their long slumber. It didn't even occur to her not to kiss him back. When you'd gone as long as she had without feeling anything but dread when it came to hooking up, you didn't question it. You just thanked your lucky stars and went with it.

And Roxxy went with it with gusto. She threw her arms around his neck, and opened her mouth wider, letting his tongue delve further into her mouth as she ran her fingers through his silky, wheat-colored hair. She even unfolded her legs so she could wrap them around his waist. It was like every part of her body needed to touch him, even her feet and toes wanted in on the action. Not to mention the part between her legs. It was on fire and throbbing, so frustrated with the layers of clothes that kept it from touching this guy that Roxxy felt a wild urge to tear off her skirt and underwear if it meant getting him inside her faster.

Apparently Andrew had the same idea. He pushed up her skirt and dug a hand past the waistband of her lace panties to cup her naked sex in his warm palm. Roxxy groaned with gratitude, even though her vagina was already telling her his big hand wasn't enough, not nearly enough...

The Wild One

"Oh God, Layla," he moaned.

Then he leaned forward and started to push her onto her back. And that's when the familiar fear spiked in her chest, and she shoved him away, saying, "No! Stop!"

Andrew immediately put his hands up in the air and backed away. "Sorry," he bit out.

Shame coursed through her entire body, hot and bitter. "Don't apologize. I'm the one who should be saying sorry. I have some issues," Roxxy mumbled.

She had sung in front of twenty thousand people just two nights ago without even a mild case of the butterflies. But she couldn't bring herself to look at her host or open her mouth to explain things, she was so embarrassed.

"Issues?" he repeated. Then his face grew hard. "I'm assuming you mean Nathan."

Once again, she didn't know how to answer.

But before she could even begin to concoct some sort of response, he said, "No, I'm the one who's sorry, Layla. I know you probably came here because I told you I'd be here for you if you ever broke up with Nathan. But that was then, and to tell you the truth, I thought you and my brother were going to go the distance."

Now Roxxy did look up at him, her eyes wide as saucers. He had been hitting on his sister-in-law, even though she was married to his brother? That was pretty messed up. And she'd thought her life had all sorts of drama. No, it looked like she'd walked right into a full-on soap opera with this one.

"Let me get this straight. You were in love, but you're not anymore?" she asked, wanting to hear the full story without giving anything away.

"Yes. No." He rubbed a hand over his face. "I chose to give you up. I chose to move on, because I thought you were happy with Nathan."

Her eyes narrowed. She lied for a living, and this guy was not doing a very good job. "Just so you know, that kiss didn't read "totally over the girl" to me."

"Dammit, Layla. I have a girlfriend." He slammed his hand down on the back of the chair. "I can't do this with you, because I have a girlfriend, okay?"

"Okaaay," Roxxy said carefully, not quite knowing what else to say at the moment, considering how angry he seemed to be at both himself and her/Layla.

"She's really nice. And she's simple, and she's what I need. I'm not going to give her up for you."

Roxxy shook her head. "I'm not asking you to give up anything or anyone for me."

That seemed to calm him down a little bit. "Good. You can stay here as long as you want. But we can't…"

Roxxy was beginning to feel more than a little annoyed by this line of conversation, even if he was really having it with this Layla person, not her. "I get it," she said. "No you and me. I'm totally cool with that. I've been trying to simplify my life, too, lately." She came up with the plan as she spoke it. "I tell you what, I'll just lay low and stay out of your way. I promise. I don't want to come between you and your really nice girlfriend."

He smiled, his mouth crooking up at the edge. "Same ol' Layla. Of course that's what you'd say. You always take the high road." He sounded more disappointed than complimentary when he said this, though.

Roxxy had to work to keep her expression neutral. She only took the high road when it suited her purposes, or when she wanted to look good for the press. But apparently this Layla was the kind of girl who would come all the way to Montana to snag a guy and then let him go as soon as he said he was already dating someone. Curious.

But she shrugged it off and got down to the brass tacks of their agreement. "So I'll stay here. It might be a while but I'll pay you back for my room and board, I promise."

"You don't have to pay me back. We're still friends, even if we're technically not family anymore. Like I said, stay as long as you want. I've got a lot of things to take care of before I go to the East Coast on business in a couple of weeks, so we probably won't be seeing each other much anyway. But if you get lonely, I've got a housekeeper who comes in to clean up and make lunch and dinner every day. She'll be happy to show you around or get you anything you need."

Good. That was great. She had a place to stay where no one knew who she really was, just like Steve Kass wanted.

So why then did she have to fake a smile when she answered, "Perfect, that sounds just perfect."

CHAPTER 6

STEVE Kass had given her his boss's number but hadn't given her his own. He'd also said on the plane that he'd stick around until the end of the week to help her get acclimated, but now he was nowhere to be found. What was going on?

As soon as Andrew was out of hearing distance, she pulled the D.A.'s business card out of her purse, which she found waiting for her on top of the dresser drawer.

"You know, you're really not supposed to be calling me, especially not from an easily traceable landline," the D.A. said after she told him who she was.

"I know, sir," she said. "But something weird has happened." She quickly ran down the whole story.

"Let me see if I've got this right," he said after she finished. "You're exactly where Steve was planning to plant you, but you're not happy about your cover story?"

"That's just it, I don't think it *is* a cover story. This guy, Andrew, is acting like I'm really his sister-in-law, some girl named Layla. I'm pretty sure he thinks we're the same person. And I'm not staying in a guest cabin like I was supposed to. He has me up in his house. It seriously feels like I've walked into an episode of *Days of Our Lives*."

"So you're saying you got drunk, woke up at the place where you're supposed to be laying low for the next few weeks anyway, and this guy basically dropped a cover story into your lap?"

"But it's not really a cover story, because he truly believes I'm this other girl."

"Sounds like a cover story to me. I say go with it."

"It's not that simple—"

"Listen, it is that simple. Lay low with the story you've been given and let us do our job," he said, sounding more than a little irritated. "Now, if you don't mind, I've got about a dozen other high profile cases on my desk right now."

"But what about Mr. Kass?" she asked. "Aren't you worried about him?"

"If he doesn't report in or show up in forty-eight hours, then I'll worry. Until then, I'm getting back to work, and I suggest you work on committing to this cover story you've been given."

"But—"

"No more buts, and don't call here again unless it's a true emergency. Especially not from a landline."

And then he hung up, leaving Roxxy to wonder exactly how such a cranky guy managed to get elected into his position in the first place.

She took a shower and found a white silk robe on the back of the bathroom door emblazoned with the words "Sinclair Ranch" across the left breast. Perfect. She'd wear this until she could wash her clothes and figure out how to ask her former "brother-in-law" for some money to buy clothes.

After coming back into the bedroom, she tried to keep herself busy, but there wasn't a television or even a radio, just a bunch of magazines and brochures, detailing all of the amenities at Sinclair Ranch which apparently consisted of horseback riding lessons, clay shooting, and even a weekly cattle drive. It was very interesting, but it took her less than an hour to get through every piece of reading material in the room. And since she didn't have her phone anymore, she couldn't even amuse herself with one of the games she used to pass the time when she was out on the road.

Her stomach grumbled, and she realized she was starving. She headed downstairs to see if she could find anything to eat. But when she arrived, she found a short, brown woman with streaks of gray running through her otherwise jet black hair, bustling around the large, open-plan galley kitchen right off the wood-paneled living room.

The woman jumped about a mile high when Roxxy walked up to the living room side of the breakfast bar and gave a tentative, "Hello."

"Sorry, sorry!" Roxxy found herself saying to yet another person that morning.

But the little Latina woman waved the apology away. "No, it is I who am sorry, Mrs. Layla. Mr. Andrew didn't tell me he was expecting guests."

But if he hadn't told his housekeeper she was here, how did she know her name? "I'm sorry, have we met before?"

"No, no we have not met." The woman wiped her hands on the dish towel with a guilty look. "But I saw your picture on the T.V. when you and Mr. Andrew were all over the news, you know, after what happened with his dead wife and before you married his brother."

Then she crossed herself.

Roxxy had to clamp her lips together to keep her mouth from dropping open. And only five minutes after deciding to full on pretend to be this Layla person, she had to fight the urge to break cover so she could get the full back story on her and Andrew. Maybe she really did look a lot like Layla if even Andrew's housekeeper could mistake her for the other woman. Moreover, if she was interpreting what the woman was saying correctly, Andrew was a widower, and something crazy had happened between his dead wife and Layla, so crazy it had

The Wild One

landed them both in the news before Layla married his brother.

"I must say I am very sorry about this terrible thing that happened to you. I know Mr. Andrew was very guilty about it afterwards. He is such a kind man, how could he not feel bad? But our God is in all things, and everything worked out. So we will not speak of it anymore. You are hungry, *si*? Sit, sit, I will make you a sandwich."

She said the last bit as if a sandwich was a cure-all for all manner of past traumas, and indicated Roxxy should sit on one of the brown leather stools at the breakfast bar.

Roxxy did as she was bid, her mind spinning. Andrew had a dead wife? And she hurt Layla in some way? And hold up, why had the housekeeper called him kind?

The man who she'd had a conversation with earlier was many things—terse, wary, and okay, let's be honest...*sexy as all get out*. But she wouldn't have labeled him kind.

As if summoned by her thoughts, Andrew came in through the kitchen door. "Hey Mrs. Garcia, I meant to tell you I've got somebody staying with me for a little bit—"

He stopped short when he saw Roxxy sitting at the breakfast bar.

His face became stony and he said, "Well, I guess you already met. I'll take my sandwich and be on my way."

Mrs. Garcia looked at him confused. "But I was just finishing up this sandwich for Mrs. Layla. I'll make another one, you can both eat down here."

"Oh, he can have that sandwich. I can wait," Roxxy said, at the same time Andrew said, "I'd prefer to eat in my office."

"No, no, sit Mr. Andrew. I am surprised at you! She is your sister-in-law and a guest. You must sit."

"No, I'll take the sandwich in my office." Andrew took

off his cowboy hat and walked through the kitchen to hang it on a hook in the living room. As he walked past, Roxxy couldn't help but notice the way his lean muscles played under the blue-and-white checked shirt he was wearing.

"Seriously, it's no problem to wait," Roxxy assured her.

As if she didn't hear either of them, Mrs. Garcia turned back to the counter and started making a second sandwich. "Two sandwiches coming right up." Then as if things weren't awkward enough, she asked. "Or should I make three? Do you think Mr. Nathan will be coming down for lunch, too?"

Silence filled the kitchen.

Then Andrew said, "Mr. Nathan isn't here. And Layla is no longer my sister-in-law, so you can drop the Mrs."

Mrs. Garcia turned back around to Roxxy, crestfallen. "I am sorry. I did not know. So just two sandwiches then."

"No," Andrew said, his voice tight. "Give me that sandwich. I'm taking it up to my office."

"But—"

"Just give it to me," Andrew bit out, only a few octaves away from yelling.

A wide-eyed Mrs. Garcia handed him the plate she had been making for Roxxy.

"Would you like some iced tea?" she asked, talking to him like a social worker would talk to a mentally unstable homeless man.

"No, I have water in the office."

And then he was gone without so much as a thank you.

"He is usually much better than this," Mrs. Garcia told her, looking like an embarrassed mother. "Mr. Andrew, you know, is a very, very kind man."

"If you say so," Roxxy answered, wondering if the woman was slightly delusional.

The Wild One

Mrs. Garcia set the glass of iced tea Andrew had rejected in front of her. "It is just he is very stressed about the Sinclair Ranch projects. He is under a lot of pressure after buying the town."

"Wait, did you just say he *bought the town?*" Roxxy asked.

"*Si*, he didn't tell you? This town was filled with dying farms and ranches before he came to here. But then he did a makeover on this old guest ranch, and now he's planning to turn the entire town into different kinds of guest ranches, so people can come from all over to visit us. So you see why he is not himself right now."

Wow, that was an ambitious project, Roxxy thought. So apparently Andrew, though he didn't look to be much older than her, had enough money to buy not only the guest ranch, but also a whole freaking town.

No wonder he wasn't worried about her paying him back.

Roxxy started to take a sip of iced tea, but then stopped. "I hate eating alone. Do you mind making two sandwiches so you can eat lunch with me? Then maybe you can tell me more about Sinclair Ranch, and Andrew's plans for the rest of the town."

CHAPTER 7

MRS. GARCIA turned out to be a great lunch date. She helped Roxxy get her clothes into the washing machine, which was located downstairs, then gave her the lowdown on Sinclair Ranch & Resort and the plans for Sinclair Township. Apparently, the Sinclair Ranch was considered a "luxury ranch," but Andrew planned to turn the rest of the town into more affordable guest ranches that vacationers under a certain income bracket could enjoy. According to Mrs. Garcia, the brochures in Roxxy's room were back from when the newly renovated ranch first opened its doors, shortly after Andrew had moved back to Montana and claimed the house as his own.

"There's much more to do now, including special summer-only activities. We added a spa last year. Or you could go on one of the nature walks or hot air ballooning. You could even take a lasso lesson if you wanted," Mrs. Garcia told her. "After your clothes finish drying, you should go to the main lodge and see the full list of activities. Don't worry about paying for anything. Just tell the front desk you're a guest of Mr. Andrew."

A guest of Mr. Andrew. Funny, she didn't feel like much of a guest. After Mrs. Garcia shooed her away so she could get back to cooking and cleaning, Roxxy gave herself a solo tour of the two-story house. There were three bedrooms on the top floor besides her own. She assumed the largest one belonged to Andrew, but she didn't dare go in there for fear of her less-than-amicable host accusing of her of snooping around. Better to wait until he and Mrs. Garcia were out of the house, she thought, then she'd snoop.

There was a fourth open door at the end of the hallway.

The Wild One

But before she could get close enough to peek inside, Andrew appeared at the doorway. "Do you need something Mrs. Garcia can't get you?" he asked, his voice surly.

Roxxy froze in her steps. "No, I was just, you know, looking around."

His jaw tightened, and he closed the door to what she assumed was his office without another word.

Guest of Mr. Andrew, indeed.

Feeling like she had no other choice, she got dressed again in her mini skirt and shimmery tank top and left the house. But as she walked the short distance to the guest ranch's main lodge, she wished she had packed something other than stilettos. She'd never gone horseback riding, but she knew from onstage experience that lassoing something while wearing high heels was a total bitch, even if it was a human dancer who was being paid to get caught by your rope.

The woman at the front desk, who was dressed in jeans and a cowboy hat, didn't exactly laugh when Roxxy asked what activities were available, but she did look like she was fighting hard not to do so when she answered, "Well, we require jeans and boots for our horseback riding classes and trail rides. But we have a lasso class starting in about fifteen minutes, and there's no dress code for that, although maybe you'd be a little more comfortable in something...well, a little more comfortable."

Roxxy looked down at her outfit, which did seem more than bit out of place. Oh well, other than the guest robe in her room, this was all she had so she'd just have to make do. If she could dance and sing for over two hours in outfits like these, a thirty-minute lasso class shouldn't kill her.

"You serious in that get-up, little gal?" the crusty old

cowboy leading the class asked when she walked over to the fenced in area where the lassoing would be taking place.

The other class participants, mostly families and all dressed in denim and cotton ensembles, were openly staring. But Roxxy, who was used to being the most outrageously dressed in the room, just shrugged. "Yep."

"Name's Jeb," the cowboy said, tipping his hat toward her. "I'm assuming you just got here."

"Actually, I'm a guest of Mr. Andrew," Roxxy answered, just like Mrs. Garcia had told her too.

The old cowboy's face lit up. "In that case, welcome, welcome. Mr. Sinclair's the most stand-up man this ranch hand's ever met. Any friend of his is a friend of mine."

Roxxy tilted her head to the side. Was this guy for real? She wondered if this was a little like how her back-up singers and dancers all claimed Roxxy was the best and most talented person they'd ever worked with in the behind-the-scenes interviews for her upcoming HBO special. "The warmest person in show business," one of them declared, even though she rarely said more than a few words to them during rehearsal and didn't talk backstage in order to preserve her voice for the performance.

But unlike those dancers, Jeb sounded completely sincere and even went so far as to declare her lassoing a post on her first try to be the by-product of her knowing Andrew. Of course she couldn't tell him she'd actually trained with a top rodeo star for several weeks to get this particular skill down.

The rest of the ranch's staff seemed to feel the same way about Andrew. The woman who led the nature walk she went on later in the afternoon had nothing but unsolicited praise for the surly man who'd closed his

51

The Wild One

office door in her face. And when she got back to his place, Mrs. Garcia went on and on about what a nice guy Mr. Andrew was, even though Roxxy had to all but force the older woman to eat dinner with her after Mrs. Garcia informed her Andrew had decided at the last minute to "go out with his Miss Amy" rather than eat dinner at the house like he usually did.

"I told him I had enough for all three of you," Mrs. Garcia said after she set down their plates. "But he just kept on saying he wanted to go out with her in Buellton—that's where she lives." A stricken look passed over her face. "You don't think Mr. Andrew has stopped liking my food, do you? He'd be too nice to tell me if I wasn't doing a good job, I know."

"Are you kidding?" Roxxy asked, her mouth full of mashed potatoes. "This meal is amazing. Andrew's crazy for not eating here."

Roxxy wasn't just trying to make the older woman feel better. This meal was way better than anything her own personal chef had ever come up with, though to be fair, her chef got paid to come up with dishes that would provide her with just enough calories to do a concert every two days and not calorie more. Eating a meal made with things like real butter and starches was nothing short of heaven to Roxxy who had gone years with only proteins and vegetables.

"And I for one am happy he decided to leave us alone. Now you can give me the dirt on him and Amy."

"Oh, Miss Amy is a very sweet girl, a very sweet girl. Mr. Andrew likes her very much."

Roxxy kept her grin pasted on, even if Mrs. Garcia's words felt a little like getting kicked in the stomach. The press had described her as a lot of things, but a "very sweet girl" had never been one of them.

"Her father is the sheriff in Buellton and Miss Amy works for one of the cattle feed companies we use. That's how she and Mr. Andrew met. They've been dating for almost a year now, and Mr. Andrew makes sure to go see her at least once or twice a week."

"Once or twice a week?" Roxxy repeated with a frown. "She never stays over?"

Mrs. Garcia giggled. "Oh no. Miss Amy is a very good girl, a very good girl. She wouldn't do that."

A very good girl. Another gut kick for another term never used in the same sentence as Roxxy's name. But out loud, she said, "Well, she sounds very nice. Andrew's lucky to have found her."

"I think he'll ask her to marry him soon. Has he said anything to you?"

Roxxy suddenly wasn't so excited about her meal anymore. She put her fork down. "No, but as you can see, he doesn't say much to me."

"Well, Mr. Andrew can be quiet," Mrs. Garcia said, quickly coming to his defense. "And you know, I was thinking about it earlier, and I decided he would never act the way he does with you unless he was still feeling guilty about what happened with his dead wife. It must be tearing him apart."

Roxxy lifted her eyebrows. "Usually if people feel guilty, they're even nicer."

"*Si*, but maybe he feels too awkward to be nice. After you married his brother, he came back here and it took him many weeks before he became the Mr. Andrew we all know and love today."

"Sure, sure," Roxxy said. "Well, I can't wait to meet that guy if he ever shows up."

After they finished dinner, Mrs. Garcia walked her over to the nearby creek, where several people were circled up around a campfire. Here she once again found Jeb, but this time he was telling spooky stories as the warm flames licked the night.

Roxxy carefully sat down on one of the logs surrounding the fire, folding her legs under at a downward angle, so as not to give anyone a show.

But she could feel the eyes of the appropriately dressed guests on her, and for the first time in a very long time, she felt uncomfortable in her wardrobe. With a sudden ache, she missed Mabel all over again. It was so hard to believe she was really gone, and that she'd never see her again.

She sent up a silent prayer that her friend was at peace and had hopefully been put on guardian angel duty, because she'd make a great one. Then she let herself enjoy the Montana night.

Unlike New York in the summer time, which could just about swelter a girl to death with all the traffic and the looming buildings throwing off sticky heat, Montana was perfect. Not too hot, with a lovely breeze passing through, making it just the right amount of comfortable as Jeb told his story.

But all too soon, the last story was told, and it was time to go. Roxxy walked back to Andrew's house alone, her shoes in one hand, and nothing but the sound of crickets to keep her company. It felt glorious. No papers to turn in. No text messages or emails to return. No large audience to keep entertained. No one telling her to stand here, do this, rehearse that. Just her and a huge expanse of starry night sky.

Her only order of business when she got home was to don the robe and throw her clothes in a washing machine so she'd have them for the next day. This time, though, she decided to hang them on the line to dry. She had no idea how long she'd be stuck in this outfit, which was technically, dry-clean only, so best not to expose it to too much heat. She chuckled as she hung the clothes on a line in Andrew's backyard, wondering what Mabel would do if she could see her now, actually taking care of her clothes as opposed to sleeping in them.

But then she felt someone's eyes on her. She turned around and caught Andrew at the window, watching her. He must have just gotten home.

She raised her hand and waved, thinking of the man that Mrs. Garcia and so many of the staff had described to her that day. But this Andrew didn't wave back. In fact, he scowled before turning away from the window. Moments later, the kitchen light flicking off was the only proof he'd ever been at the window at all.

CHAPTER 8

TELLING Layla she could stay as long as she wanted had been a mistake, and Andrew was kicking himself for it. It had only been one day, but having her in such close proximity was driving him crazy and he couldn't understand why.

Even when they'd dated in college, he'd had no problem being a complete gentleman with her. He'd respected that she was a virgin and hadn't pressured her to consummate their relationship, even though he wouldn't have minded taking their make-out sessions further. He hadn't cared that she was black or from a much poorer background. She was unlike any other girl he'd ever dated, and he just wanted to be with her.

Even after she'd left town, he'd thought of her more fondly than lustfully. And when she'd shown up in Pittsburgh years later, soon after he'd decided to divorce his wife, he had hoped for a fresh start between them. That she'd chosen his brother once again over him had stuck in his craw, but he'd done the honorable thing and blessed their union, even stood up for Nathan at their wedding. However, it had taken months of building up the Sinclair Ranch before he was able to truly be happy for them.

He had decided he and Layla had been better friends than lovers. He had decided she made his brother a better man and their marriage would thrive. He had decided he wanted her to be happy and he should move on.

So why then had he been hard as a rock all day? Why couldn't he even be in the same room with her without his dick jumping in his pants, practically begging its master to take her right then and there?

Layla had changed. The last time he'd seen her, she'd

been just as gentle and sweet as the college girl he remembered. But the Layla he'd found stumbling through the parking lot had an edge to her. It wasn't just the alcohol. It was something else, the way she wore her uncharacteristic mini skirt like it was a work uniform as opposed to wildly inappropriate. The shrewd, knowing look that came over her face when she told him his kiss "didn't read 'totally over the girl.'"

And then there was the way her slightly rounded hips moved underneath the skirt whenever she walked. At least the robe left something to the imagination. Watching her walk in stilettos to the main lodge from his office window had nearly sent him over the edge. His dick had gotten so hard as he imagined all the ways he might fuck her. Not make love to her, but fuck her hard and strong like a disease he was trying to get out of his system. Nothing like the soft-toned boyhood fantasies from their college years. No, now he wanted to ravage and consume her in a few ways that might not be strictly legal in the state of Montana.

That night he saw a glimpse of a breast underneath her guest robe as she was hanging her clothes to dry. Afterward, he'd had to take himself in his own hand. And even though he tried to imagine Amy as he worked his cock, as soon as he closed his eyes it had been all Layla, bending over in her mini skirt and smiling back at him, bidding him do whatever he wanted to do to her naked pussy, which he'd discovered this morning was completely bald, as if she had shaved it all off in anticipation of seeing him.

He cursed as streams of hot cum erupted all over his hand and hoped that would be it. But then the house creaked, which let him know she was still up and moving around downstairs, probably still dressed in that thin robe.

His dick instantly became hard again.

Yes, letting Layla stay had been a mistake. A big, big mistake.

ROXXY REALLY ENJOYED RANCH LIFE. By day two she'd not only lassoed a pig all by herself, but had taken two more nature walks and spent much of the day with the children's program, making Native American arts and crafts, playing croquet and Frisbee, and learning how to fly fish.

Most of the adults at the ranch seemed perfectly happy to leave their kids to their own activities while they enjoyed the ranch's spa and other amenities. Roxxy assumed this must be because they'd had actual childhoods, unlike her who had been lazily homeschooled by her mother so she could spend as much time as possible going from one singing audition to another.

Roxxy had been grateful when she got her first record contract at sixteen because the label had provided her with a real teacher who actually taught her things. But she'd never been able to do the really fun stuff like arts and crafts or play games with other children, and she found herself more than enjoying her time with the children's program.

If the other staff members thought her continued presence strange, they didn't acknowledge it, maybe because she was a "guest of Mr. Andrew" or maybe because she played so hard with the kids, it actually made their jobs easier. And the one nice thing about racial stereotyping was that most of the parents seemed way more comfortable with the strangely dressed black woman in a service position as opposed to as a fellow guest. A few of them even gave her friendly hellos at dinner that night.

Mrs. Garcia informed her during their lunch together that Andrew made it a point to eat with the staff in the main lodge on Wednesdays. "But I can stay and cook you dinner again if you want."

"No, no," she said. "I can eat at the main lodge, too."

However, when she got to the staff table with her plate filled with all sorts of yummy-looking food from the country-style buffet, she began to see the holes in her plan. The rest of the staff greeted her warmly and assured her it was totally fine to sit with them. They even made room for her on the bench, so she could sit between Andrew and Elena, the woman who ran the children's program.

However, for quite a few moments after she sat down, Andrew looked like he was fighting the impulse to take his plate and get up from the table. But then he reset, apparently having made the calculated decision to act like he wasn't repulsed by her presence. Instead, he proceeded to ignore her for the entire meal.

Strangely enough, Roxxy didn't mind because that was how she finally came to meet the other Andrew, the one everyone at the ranch had been raving about. Over dinner he was charming and engaged, asking after many of the staff-members' children and listening attentively to any problems they were having in their positions. By the time he had cleared his plate, he'd agreed to stop by the stables to make a hard decision about one of the older horses and also speak with a guest who kept insisting on pinching the butts of the female wait staff whenever they brought him drinks.

When he got up to leave, so did Roxxy, but he chose that moment to speak to her for the first time that day. "No, stay. Try the peach cobbler. It's the best in Montana. Best in the nation I think, but officially it's only been awarded the prize for best in state."

The Wild One

The staff around the table laughed at his little joke, and they called out a chorus of hearty good nights as he left. But Roxxy knew better. The invitation to try dessert had been another slight on his part, even if no one else could see it.

Still, she rallied after he was gone and got to talking to Elena about the children's program.

"I'd loved to have come out here when I was kid," Roxxy told her.

"Me too," Elena said. "I'm just sad more kids can't afford the opportunity. But that's why Andrew's headed to Washington D.C. in a couple of weeks. He's got a few grant meetings about turning the old Hagstead farm into a summer camp for underprivileged kids. But he's having a heck of time getting ready for them. Last week he said just getting through the paperwork to get non-profit status for the farm has been way more complicated than he expected."

Roxxy's eyes lit up. "Really? I was actually thinking about going to school for public administration, which involves a lot of non-profit course work."

Jeb frowned. "I thought you were a physical therapist. That's what all the newspapers said."

Roxxy lifted her eyebrows. So that was what the mysterious Layla did for a living.

"Um, yeah, I am," she said. "But lately I've been thinking about changing career paths."

Jeb nodded with sage understanding. "Was a lawyer myself in Helena, before I accepted the call of the wild."

Roxxy smiled. "Cool! Then you'll have to tell me how you did it. I need all the advice I can get."

As it turned out, a lot of the staff had done other things before coming to Sinclair Ranch. "The hotel industry can be like that, attracting people from all different walks of life," Elena, who taught fourth grade in Buellton during the school year, told her. "But you know that already, since Andrew was still an executive at Sinclair Steel when everything went down between you and his wife."

A hush came over the table and everyone seemed to be shooting eye daggers at Elena. Apparently they'd all been talking about whatever happened between Layla and Andrew's dead wife behind her back, but it wasn't considered polite to actually bring it up to "Layla" herself.

"Yeah, he was," Roxxy said, trying to lighten the mood. "But I don't want to take *that* big of a leap. I was thinking about maybe finding some rich rock star to work for and doing some charitable foundation work."

This was actually mostly true. They just didn't realize *she* was the rich rock star and that the money for her foundation would be coming out of her own coffers.

That seemed to bring back the former mood and people started talking about what charitable things they would do if they had rock star money.

All in all, it turned out to be a nice dinner, and it was even nicer to have people to sit with at that night's bonfire. But all too soon, it became time for her to walk home barefoot and alone.

She once again washed her outfit and hung it up on the line. When she came back to the house, she spotted Andrew's cowboy hat hanging on its hook in the living room, which meant he'd once again arrived while she was outside. But this time, he hadn't bothered to come to the window or even say good night.

Whatever. Roxxy pushed the insult away and went into the kitchen to make some warm tea, which she'd learned the night before to drink alone. It had taken three cups just to calm down enough to attempt sleeping in her bedroom. And after hours of fitful dozing, she'd had a nightmare about Steve Kass. In it, he was lying on the floor with blood coming out his mouth and nose, just like Mabel. She'd come awake on the edge of a scream. There had been no getting back to sleep after that.

And as jittery as she was feeling at the moment, she doubted that night would be any better as far as convincing herself to attempt sleep again was concerned.

Except that night, Andrew showed up at the living room entrance to the kitchen about two hours into her nighttime pacing session, while she was making her fourth cup of tea.

"What are you doing?" he asked from the doorway, sounding more like he was making an accusation than asking a question.

"I love Montana, but I'm having trouble sleeping here," she answered. "I think it's the crickets."

"This house is old, leftover from before the renovations. When you move around down here I can hear you upstairs."

"Sorry," Roxxy said. "I'll just take my tea up to my bedroom."

"And what happens if you still can't get to sleep?"

"Then I come back down here and make myself another cup of tea, I guess. Maybe try and read a book, since there's no television or internet here. I'm not really used to not having something to do at night."

His eyes clouded over at that. "You miss your old life."

"No," Roxxy said, though she was aware they were talking about two different things entirely. "I don't miss my old life at all. It's just that Montana is really dark and crickety. Not what I'm used to."

He gave his head a tired shake. "I've got a conference call first thing tomorrow morning. I'm not going to let you keep me up all night, again. I need to be on the ball."

"I wasn't trying to keep you up," Roxxy said through gritted teeth. "Just let me get my cup of tea and I'll—"

He turned off the stove and took her by the arm. "Come on," he said.

"Where are we going?" she asked.

He didn't answer, but their destination was soon revealed when he opened the door to the master bedroom. This bedroom was much larger than the one he'd given her, with furniture made out of the same material as the old-fashioned barn, which Jeb had told her was used to store hay for the horses and feed for the cows.

"I was like you when I first got here, after leaving my wife," Andrew said, after indicating she should go into the room ahead of him. "I knew our marriage wasn't working, but I couldn't get to sleep at first because I was used to having somebody else in bed with me."

"That is definitely not why I can't get to sleep," Roxxy assured him. If only he knew how long it had been since she'd had anyone in her bed overnight.

"Just lay down," he said. "I'll stay on my side, you can stay on yours. If you're not asleep within an hour, then feel free to go downstairs, make more tea, and resume your pacing."

Roxxy frowned. "Just an hour? Then no more complaining if I need a few more cups of teas to fall asleep?"

"If you're not asleep within an hour, I'll escort you to the liquor cabinet and pour you a glass of scotch myself. That's how I eventually started getting to sleep on my own."

"I don't really drink. Two nights ago was fluke," Roxxy said.

But she tentatively climbed into the left side of the bed, getting as close to the edge as she could before she let the sheet settle over her.

"But if this means I can go back to making my tea in peace…" she said. Then she closed her eyes so Andrew wouldn't be able to accuse her of not at least giving it the old college try.

She never got her fourth cup of tea. And the next thing she knew, she was having some kind of weird sex dream. In it, she was lying on her side and grinding her naked hips against someone's very large erection.

"Let me in, Layla."

"Take off your pants," she gasped out, barely able to contain herself.

But he didn't take them off, just kept grinding his hips against hers, until she thought she might go crazy with lust.

"Layla, wake up."

"Please," she cried. "I want you inside of me. I'm going to come if you don't take off your pants."

"Layla…stop."

But she couldn't stop her hips from seeking out what they so desperately wanted, and soon she felt herself shatter against his cloth-covered erection. She moaned as her dream orgasm rippled through her, riding her body in waves.

The sensations were so intense they jerked her awake with a loud gasp. And that was when she discovered it hadn't been a dream. She was in Andrew's arms, and his gray eyes were open, boring into hers with unbridled anger. Also, from what she could feel, she had just come all over the crotch of his pajama pants.

CHAPTER 9

ANDREW had never had a dream like this. In it, he and Layla were laying sideways in his bed, kissing, and everything else had fallen away: the ranch, Nathan, Amy—nothing else mattered but their joining together.

He ground his hips against hers, but though they were both completely naked, some invisible force was keeping him from what he wanted the most. To be balls deep inside of her, fucking her the way that sweet body of hers had been tempting him to ever since she showed up in Sinclair Township.

"Let me in, Layla," he groaned.

"Take off your pants," she answered back, even though he wasn't wearing any.

Andrew came awake in a blaze of hot confusion, only to find an even hotter sight in front of him: Layla, her guest robe open to reveal her tight brown body, was grinding against him in the wild throes of a sex dream.

Even as his dick rejoiced and demanded he do exactly what she'd asked, his conscience let him know no matter how unbelievably sexy she was at the moment, he couldn't plunge himself into somebody who wasn't awake, somebody who wasn't his girlfriend.

"Layla, wake up," he said, hating the reluctance he heard in his own voice.

Please," she cried, still writhing against him with her eyes closed. "I want you inside of me. I'm going to come if you don't take off your pants."

His dick was thrumming, he wanted her so bad. "Layla ... stop," he said, but he was barely able to get out the words, his voice was so clogged with lust.

Then she came, so hard her climax soaked through the

crotch of his pants. And that was what finally woke her up in the end.

Her big eyes flew open, and she looked six different kinds of stricken as she realized what had happened.

Andrew's heart iced over. "You thought I was Nathan, didn't you?"

"No!" But still she scrambled away from him, sitting up in the bed and closing her robe as if something horrific had just happened. "I've never done anything like that in my life. I thought—I thought it was a dream, but I definitely thought it was you in the dream. I'm sorry. I didn't mean to—"

"Stop fucking apologizing to me," he said angrily, unable to bear the contrition in her voice, as if doing anything intimate with him was the worst thing on earth.

That's when it occurred to him. "You didn't come here because of me, did you? You came here because you knew this would be the last place on Earth anyone, including Nathan, would look for you. That's why you took the bus into town as opposed to a plane, because you could pay in cash. You're hiding out here."

Her eyes flashed with guilt before she looked away and that told him all he needed to know.

"Say something," he said, his voice low and dangerous.

"Like what?" she shouted back. She stood up and firmly tied the robe's belt around her waist. "You told me to stop fucking apologizing to you."

For a moment, Andrew was taken aback. He'd never heard Layla curse, even in the heat of anger. Then the moment passed and she was suddenly on the move.

"You don't want me to say I'm sorry, but I am. I really am. I shouldn't have done that, and I shouldn't have come here. You don't understand, I'm not who you think."

"I know you're not. The Layla I knew would never use

one brother to hide from another. You know, I've always thought you were the innocent victim where Nathan and I were concerned. He came after you because you were dating me. I was to blame for letting him believe you didn't want to be with him after your accident. And after what Diana tried to do to you, I was eaten alive with guilt. It would have killed me if something had happened to you because of what I'd done. But right now, the way you're acting, like you're as hot for me as you used to be for Nathan? I'm seriously wondering if you haven't been playing us against each other from day one."

Her eyes widened with the insult and she opened her mouth to say something back. But then at the last moment, she clapped her hand over her mouth and ran out the room.

Andrew cursed silently as he watched her go.

AFTER THE ARGUMENT WITH ANDREW, Roxxy ran straight out of the house. Didn't even bother to get her shoes. Just grabbed the same clothes she had been wearing for three days straight off the line and walked down the ranch's main dirt road until she came upon the old gray barn where they stored the hay and other feed. She pulled open one of its double doors, grateful for the refuge. She then put on her clothes before putting the robe back on and curling up in a fetal position on a hay bale.

She'd once had a nip slip on the red carpet that made the front covers of several European gossip mags. She'd flubbed the American national anthem in front of millions of World Series viewers. There was even a viral video going around of her falling on her butt at a concert, an animated gif of which had been turned into a popular meme people liked to leave in the comment sections of articles about people saying or doing stupid things.

But she had never been as embarrassed as she was after sleep humping Andrew. How the hell did she let that happen? She'd been called frigid by more than one guy who hadn't been able to bust through her reserve and get into her pants. How did she go from that to creaming all over some dude in her sleep? What was wrong with her?

She had to get out of here, she decided. She couldn't take living in that house with Andrew Sinclair one more minute. She didn't care what it took, she needed to get off this ranch. Like right now, before she went crazy with lust and confusion. She'd call the D.A.'s office first thing, as soon as she worked up the courage to go back to the house.

Eventually, the adrenaline from what happened that morning faded, and sleep overtook her. But the next thing she knew, someone was shaking her awake.

"Shirelle?" she said, blinking against the sunlight now flooding through the open barn door.

But no, it wasn't her mother, it was Andrew, looking even grimmer than usual. He had the straps of her heels looped under the first two fingers of his left hand.

"Who's Shirelle?" he asked.

"Nobody," she answered, sitting up on the bale of hay. "What are you doing here?"

"One of the hands called the house, asking if there was a reason you were in the barn," he answered. "C'mon."

He tossed her shoes at her.

"Where are we going?" she asked.

"Into Buellton. Jeb's already there, picking up feed for the horses, but one of our generators just went out, so I'm driving it in," he answered. He gave her an up and down look. "Plus, I'm sick of watching you flounce around here in that mini skirt. It's distracting the hands, and it's not the kind of look the Sinclair Ranch is going for, especially if you're going to be working with the children's program.

You need some decent shoes, too."

Her cheeks burned, not only because he thought she had been purposely flaunting herself, but also because— "I don't have any money on me. Not even a credit card."

"Let me guess, you're afraid to use your credit cards because you don't want Nathan to track you down here?"

She looked away. She didn't know this Nathan guy, but she was already sick of hearing his name. "Something like that," she mumbled.

"You know he's on vacation, right?" Andrew asked. "That's what Nathan does when he gets hurt. He runs away. He never even looked for you all those years you spent recovering and getting your education. Why do you think he'd look for you now?"

The bombs Andrew kept dropping about his and Layla's back story were excruciating. Seriously, the most excruciating thing she had ever endured, including her thirty days of mandatory house arrest. She vowed to look the whole story up as soon as she got reassigned to another place to lay low, hopefully this one would have internet access.

But now she just answered. "I really don't want to talk about Nathan anymore." Totally true.

He gave her a thin smile. "Of course you don't. C'mon anyway. I'll buy you whatever you need."

Wondering if she'd ever be able to go more than five minutes without feeling completely humiliated by this man, she said through gritted teeth, "I'll pay you back as soon as I can. And when we get back from town, I'll figure out some other living arrangement and get out of your hair. I promise."

He stared at her for a long, hard time, but didn't say anything. In the end, he turned and walked out the door, apparently trusting her to follow, which she did as soon as she got her stilettos back on.

Pride be damned. She was willing to do anything to get out of wearing these heels everywhere she went. Even spend more time with a man who really seemed to out-and-out hate her.

CHAPTER 10

Roxxy thought she'd do anything to get out of her stilettos, but that was before she was informed she'd have to squeeze in next to Andrew in his old candy-red pickup truck, since the generator was already sitting in the window seat. Apparently, it had broken down while the ranch hands had been mending fences, so now the back of the truck was filled with new posts and barbwire, making it so the generator had to sit up front with them.

"How far is it to Buellton?" she asked him when he got in next to her, the side of his body flush with hers.

"About an hour," he answered.

Roxxy clasped her hands tight in her lap, hoping that would be enough to mask the shiver that went through her entire body, right before she bit back against a rising panic attack.

She eventually managed to breathe her way back to normal and calm herself down, but then without warning. Andrew's hand brushed her knee. She jumped in her seat, letting out a yelp of scared surprise.

Andrew raised his hand up. "Sorry, I was just trying to turn on the radio. It's quiet in here."

"Oh," she said, her cheeks hot with embarrassment. "Let me."

She pushed the on/off button on the old-fashioned radio and a country song poured out.

"You can change it if you want," he said.

"No," she answered, going back to her tightly-folded hands position. "I like country music."

"Really," he said. "Because I remember you not caring for it much when we were in college."

"Maybe it's an acquired taste," she answered carefully.

The Wild One

"I started liking it later on."

"Seriously?" he said.

"Yes, seriously," she answered. "Are people not allowed to change their music tastes?"

Andrew threw her a skeptical look. "If you like country music so much, who's this singing?" he asked.

"Colin Fairgood," she answered. "Best songwriter in the country business, and he's one of my favorite singers right now, period."

Andrew nodded. "Mine, too. I like all his stuff, even that one duet he did with whatshername was okay. You know, that one singer who wears all the crazy outfits and makeup?"

"Roxxy RoxX?" she supplied, trying to keep her voice as level as possible.

"Yeah, that one," he said. "She has a pretty good voice. Too bad she went right back to the bubblegum. I liked when she was actually singing about something that mattered."

"Well, you can't make a career singing songs about the disenfranchised. She took a big chance, even recording that song with Colin. And I bet she's still sort of surprised it did so well on the charts."

"I wonder why he decided to do a duet with her of all people?" Andrew said.

"I don't know," Roxxy answered, because she'd wondered the same thing after she got the call from his people. "He's kind of a strange guy. I think I read in an interview or something that he just 'knew' she'd be right for the song."

"Hmm," Andrew said. Then thankfully dropped the subject.

He didn't say anything else until they got to the repair shop where Jeb was waiting for them outside to take the generator in to the mechanic.

"We'll leave the truck here with Jeb and walk on down to the general store. It's not far."

Roxxy nodded her agreement. And to her surprise, when she looked down at her hands, she found them relaxed and unfolded on her lap.

AFTER DROPPING THE GENERATOR OFF with Jeb, Andrew walked Roxxy over to the general store. But the camaraderie they'd achieved on the ride over must have faded in the wind, because he all but snapped at her, "You've got thirty minutes to pick out something decent to wear—jeans, t-shirts, and at least one long-sleeved shirt, if you're wondering what appropriate ranch wear is. Shorts are okay, too, but the kind that come down to your knees, no short-shorts or mini skirts. Now what size shoe do you wear?"

She told him. Her dad had died when she was very young, but she had a feeling this was what girls felt like when being given instructions by someone who obviously didn't approve of their current wardrobe choices.

"I'll go get you some real shoes and meet you outside the dressing room. Thirty minutes," he said again, before walking away.

His tone had been so high-handed, it was all she could do not to walk out of the store then and there, and call the D.A. again. She grumbled under her breath as she grabbed a handful of v-neck t-shirts, jeans, and cotton underwear in from the store's small selection of women's clothing.

She wished she could tell him there were literally over a million people who would be thrilled to have her as a guest in their homes. In almost every country on Earth. She never dropped the, "Do you know who I am?" bomb, but she was sorely tempted to at the moment, especially knowing she wouldn't be living off his hospitality much longer.

However, just a few minutes later, she had completely changed her mind. Whatever humiliation she had suffered, whatever kicks to her pride she had endured at the hands of this man—it no longer mattered. Because blue jeans, she discovered, were nothing short of a revelation. They were so comfortable, allowing her to bend and walk however she pleased without the constant fear of exposing herself. And cotton bras? Why hadn't anyone ever told her about cotton bras?!?! For over fifteen years, her breasts had been pushed up and pushed in by silk and underwire contraptions that felt more like torture devices than underwear. But this magical cotton bra somehow gave her support and freedom at the same time.

She all but floated out of the dressing room, feeling like a brand new woman—or at least one who was completely comfortable for the first time in her adult life.

"This outfit is amazing," she declared to Andrew, spinning around with her arms spread out. "These jeans! I have never worn something more comfortable on my body. Never ever."

He raised an eyebrow. "More comfortable than scrubs?"

Oh yeah, she had forgotten Layla was supposed to be a physical therapist. "I have never worn something that looks this good *and* is this comfortable in my life. What brand are these? They're like magic!"

"They're just Levi's."

"*Then Levi's are magic*," she insisted.

To her surprise, he actually cracked a smile. "If I had known how happy a simple pair of Levi's would make you, I might have bought you some sooner."

She shook her head. "Not a simple pair. Five simple pairs please. I really don't want to wear anything but these jeans for the rest of my life. I'm totally serious about this."

He looked at her with that quizzical look again.

"What?" she asked, once again feeling self-conscious.

"You've changed," he said. "I mean, you just seem different. That's all."

Roxxy had never felt guilty about pretending she was a crazy and uninhibited rock star, when in truth, she could barely bring herself to have sex with a man. And she'd been pretending for years to have the same carefree party girl persona she put on for all of her videos, giving one giggling and vacuous interview after another.

But standing there with Andrew, who was smiling down at her like he was seeing the real her for the first time and liking what he saw, caused an unfamiliar guilt to worm its way into her heart.

"People change," she told him, looking away. "Especially if jeans are involved. You've got to admit, they're a very powerful incentive."

"Because they're magic," he said, grinning.

"Because they're totally magic," she said, grinning back at him, even though she was definitely no longer talking about the jeans.

"Andrew? Andrew is that you?"

They both looked up to see a pretty blond in a cute little sundress headed their way. She smiled and waved at them with sunshiney enthusiasm.

"Hey, honey poo," she said, giving Andrew a peck on the lips when she reached them. "

She then turned to Roxxy with an even brighter smile. "And you must be Layla. I'm so happy to meet you, although, of course I wish it had been under better circumstances." She laid a hand on her chest. "I was really

The Wild One

sorry to hear about the divorce, and after all you two had been through."

That was it, she was going to find her way to a computer so she could look up the Layla-Andrew story if it was the last thing she did. But out loud she said, "You know what they say. All good things come to an end."

Amy strung an arm around Andrew's waist. "Well, hopefully not *all* good things." She wiggled her cute little nose up at Andrew. "What are you two doing here anyway? You didn't tell me you were coming into town."

"It was a last minute trip. Layla lost her luggage on the way out here and she needed some extra clothes."

"So you took her shopping? How sweet! You're so sweet." She turned to Roxxy. "Isn't he sweet?"

"That's what everyone says," Roxxy answered, working hard to keep a smile on her face. It was like having a conversation with someone who was her exact opposite. Someone wholesome and kind, who didn't have any secrets or sexual hang-ups. Roxxy could understand exactly what attracted Andrew to her, and she couldn't blame him one bit for wanting this girl over Layla, with whom he apparently had a drama-filled past.

"But you should have called me," Amy said. "I would have been happy to take Layla shopping."

"We're almost done," Andrew answered. "Do you want to have lunch?"

Amy's face lit up, like he had made her entire day with a lunch invitation. "Sure! We can all go over to Grandma's Cafe. They've got rhubarb and strawberry pie as the dessert special today."

Having not been allowed to do so much as look sideways at a dessert for many years now, the mention of pie should have had Roxxy salivating. But just the thought of watching Andrew and Amy make googly eyes at each other for another hour killed any appetite she might have had.

"Actually, I'm not that hungry," she said,

At the same Andrew said, "Layla has some stuff she wanted to do back at the ranch."

They both stopped. Andrew to be polite, and Roxxy because she was shocked he had been so quick to disinvite her. It almost made her want to say she didn't have to get back to ranch, and was, in fact, now starving.

But Andrew didn't give her a chance. He handed her a pair of hiking boots. "Get whatever else you need and tell them to put it on the Sinclair Ranch's tab. After that, go back over to the repair shop. Jeb can give you a ride back to Sinclair."

Then without so much as a "see you later," he guided Amy away with a hand on her back, like she was precious cargo and he was trying to get her out of the reach of the ugly troll he'd come here with.

She watched them walk away. Amy and Andrew. Andrew and Amy. The perfect couple.

Roxxy was shaking with fury by the time the general store clerk finished ringing up all of her purchases. And the jeans she had been so elated about earlier definitely no longer felt like magic.

"YOU ARE NOT CALLING ME FROM a land line again," said the D.A. a few minutes later.

"It's a pay phone about an hour outside of where I'm staying, and believe me, I wouldn't be doing it, if the situation hadn't become untenable. You need to reassign me. Now. Tomorrow at the latest."

"It doesn't work like that. You're not officially part of any witness protection program, so we can't hand you over

The Wild One

to the Feds. We'd have to find someplace to stash you, and since I'm without an assistant D.A. at the moment, I don't have time to do that."

"Wait, you still haven't found him?" Roxxy asked.

"Not exactly. We traced his cell back to some motel called the Ride 'Em Cowboy, but he still hasn't called in, and it's been forty-eight hours, so tomorrow we'll be sending a team out to Montana to look for him."

"Well, while they're out here, can they come pick me up, too?"

"No, because officially, they don't even know you're out there and like I said, we have no place to put you up at the moment. Forgive me if we're more concerned about finding the assistant D.A. of New York than making sure your hotel is up to your standards."

"It's not a hotel, it's some guy's home. And it's not about a lack of amenities. I actually really like the place. But the guy I'm staying with…"

"Has he done something to you? Tried to harm you in some way."

"No, but he's cold."

"He's cold?" the district attorney repeated.

"Yeah, and he's not very nice. Everybody else thinks he is, but he's not when it comes to me."

"So let me get this straight. You want us to relocate you because your host, who doesn't know you're a celebrity, isn't fawning all over you?"

Roxxy frowned. When he put it that way it did sound a little petty. And she doubted explaining how he had just ditched her to go have lunch with his girlfriend would impress the D.A. much either.

"He thinks I'm somebody else. Somebody I'm not. And I'm tired of lying to him," she confessed.

"From what I can see, you've done nothing but pretend

to be somebody you really weren't for years now."

"Yeah, but this is different."

"How so? Because your life and well-being are at stake as opposed to your record sales?" The D.A. sighed. "Listen, Ms. RoxX, I don't particularly like your music and right now I'm not liking you very much. We have an important missing person on our hands. And we are doing everything we can to solve your case as quickly as possible. All we need you to do is cooperate for a little while longer. Prove you're not the brat the press has painted you out to be and stay put. Do that one thing for me, okay?"

Well, Roxxy felt thoroughly chastised. "Okay, I'll stay put," she said, now feeling very bad for making another unsanctioned call for what was beginning to seem like really frivolous reasons on her part. "I'm sorry. I hope you find Mr. Kass soon, and I wish I could be more help on that front."

"Me, too," he said. Then he hung up before she could ask him any more questions, including the one she had about sending money, so she could pay Andrew back.

CHAPTER 11

THE only good thing about getting ditched by Andrew Sinclair was that it alleviated some of the guilt surrounding the fact that Roxxy was lying to him and everyone who worked at the Sinclair Ranch & Resort about who she really was. So what if Andrew bought her jeans and if everyone at the ranch was being super nice to her because they thought she'd just gotten divorced?

She knew from experience they'd turn positively slavish if they knew who she really was, treating her like some kind of royalty as opposed to another woman who'd gotten divorced just like fifty percent of the married women in this country. And who cared if Andrew bought her some jeans and seemed to really appreciate how happy she was to receive them? It hadn't been out of any sense of altruism on his part. He had pretty much said he was sick of her walking around his ranch looking like a harlot. Then he'd ditched her for his perfect girlfriend as soon as she was properly covered up.

Luckily for her, the car ride back with Jeb wasn't too uncomfortable. His window seat was generator free, and he was old enough to be her grandfather. Instead of turning on the radio, he launched into a story about how his great-great-great-grandparents had come over from Europe, but ended up traveling west until they found a land of plenty, one they knew they wanted to stay in.

"That's why you got to be careful of the Montana summer. It's so beautiful this time a year, makes me people want to stay forever and the generations after them, too. Of course, it helps that their son, my great-great-grandfather met himself a Crow girl right round the time he turned seventeen. That girl ended up becoming my great-great-grandmother, and her Montana story goes back even further."

Roxxy began to relax again. Jeb was more likely to talk her ear off, than try to get fresh with her, and even then she wouldn't mind. His unending treasure chest of stories was worth a lost ear.

When she got back to the ranch, Elena and the other two women working with the children's program greeted her with pleasant surprise, complimenting her on her new outfit. "Looks like you're really one of us now," Elena said.

And for the rest of the afternoon, Roxxy did feel like one of them. It was so much easier to play with children when you didn't have to worry about flashing them if you squatted the wrong way. She spent the afternoon playing right along side the kids, doing cartwheels, playing badminton, and even a game of freeze tag.

However, her good mood faded when she came back to the house and found a note on the kitchen counter from Mrs. Garcia.

"Mr. Andrew called and told me not to worry about dinner," it said. *"See you tomorrow."*

It was easy enough to eat dinner in the cafeteria at the staff table again, but a black cloud hovered over her head. One she soon began to recognize as another unfamiliar feeling: jealousy.

She, Roxxy RoxX, who had always prided herself on not getting catty with other music stars or needing to be the center of attention wherever she went, was jealous of a sweet country girl who was pretty as the day was long and deserved nothing less than the perfect boyfriend.

Also, there was the problem of what happened the night before. She doubted the nightmares would conveniently take a night off, but she didn't dare try pacing around the house like one of the ghosts of girlfriends past again. She couldn't bear the thought of embarrassing herself like she had the last time with Andrew.

So after the campfire circle broke up, she made the trek out to the hay barn. There she curled up with a blanket she'd requested from the front desk and the new book she'd bought along with her clothes at the general store.

The romance novel was just what she needed, a very simple story with a sweet Amish girl and no chance of any blazing hot sex scenes to remind her of what happened with Andrew that morning.

Soon her eyes drifted closed and…

Steve Kass was staring up at her with blood streaming from his mouth, nose, and eye sockets.

She sat up with a gasp, only to find the barn now bathed in moonlight.

And Andrew Sinclair standing in the doorway.

"WHAT ARE YOU DOING HERE?" she asked him. She was breathing hard, and Andrew had to wonder if it was because she'd had a nightmare or because he'd frightened her with his sudden appearance.

"I think the question is what are *you* doing here?" he asked.

She seemed to think about that but then screwed up her face in that way of hers and answered, "No, I'm pretty sure my original question still stands."

Again with that uncharacteristic sass. The Layla he remembered would already be apologizing all over the place for not leaving a note and for sleeping in his barn without permission. Again. Not only did this new version of Layla not apologize, but she was also looking at him like he should be the one apologizing.

"Why weren't you at the house?" he asked her.

"I thought it would be better if I slept out here," she said.

"Why did you think that?"

"Because I didn't want to keep you up all night again with my pacing," she answered carefully, like he was a clueless for even asking the question in the first place.

"Layla," he said. Then he bit off angrily, before continuing. "I don't like the way you make me feel."

She stood up and looked at him with real curiosity in her eyes. "I wasn't aware I made you feel anything."

"Bullshit. You have to know. You're lying."

Again with that careful look, like she was running every word through some kind of check before she opened her mouth. "I'm getting that you don't like me and for some reason I irritate the hell out of you and you'd rather not be around me and probably wish I never came here in the first place." Her voice broke on the last sentence. "And believe me, I'm really wishing the same thing right now."

"Then why did you come here?" he asked her.

"I didn't have anywhere else to go," she answered.

"Bullshit," he said again. "Everybody loves you. You've got friends all over the country. That girl from Texas who married Alexei Romanov? He's a billionaire. He could have stashed you some place where Nathan never would have found you."

She looked a little confused, like this line of reasoning really hadn't occurred to her.

He came to stand directly in front of her, so close he could feel the tension emanating off her body, like she was fighting hard within herself to stand her ground and not turn tail and run. "Are you saying to me it never occurred to you to try to ask Alexei Romanov for help?"

"Yes, that's exactly what I'm saying," she answered. "Why didn't it occur to you?"

She shook her head, her brown eyes sad in the moonlight. "I'm not sure how you want me to answer that."

He stepped even closer, so close he could feel her breasts against his chest. "I want you to say you came here for me."

Her bottom lip trembled, but she didn't look away this time. "If you want me to say it, I'll say it. I came here for you," she whispered.

He brought his head closer so that his lips were hovering right above hers. "I want you to say that you came all over my dick this morning, because you wanted to fuck me, not because you thought you were in bed with Nathan."

"I told you that already," she said.

"Tell me again."

"I..." she paused, as if gathering up the courage to say what she did next. "I did what I did this morning because I wanted you. Not Nathan. You, even though I know you have a girlfriend."

"I broke up with Amy," he said.

"What?" she said, her eyes widening.

"That's why I didn't come back for dinner. She was upset. It took a while for her to calm down and I had to keep explaining and re-explaining everything to her."

"What did you tell her?" Layla asked, her voice a near whisper.

"At first I tried to tell her the usual. It wasn't her, it was me. I just didn't think I should be in a relationship with her right now. I tried not to hurt her feelings. But she's not dumb. She asked me if there was somebody else and you know I don't lie anymore. I told her I didn't want to cheat on her or disrespect her in any way and that was why I was leaving.

"She guessed it was you. I suppose it was easy, considering our history. Then there were a bunch more questions. How could I after you chose your brother over me? And what would I do if you and Nathan got back together? Then she wanted to know what you had that she didn't?'

"And what did you say," she asked.

"I didn't say anything," he answered. "I just let her keep on asking questions. I didn't tell her how I didn't mind waiting until marriage with her, but how I can barely control myself when you walk into a room. I didn't tell her how I want you more in these hiking boots and jeans than I ever wanted her in her pretty little sundresses. I didn't tell her how all I've been thinking about is fucking you since you came to the ranch. I didn't tell her about you coming all over me this morning or how it made me so crazy, I nearly fucked you right there without a condom, girlfriend or not. I just told her I couldn't be her boyfriend anymore."

Then Andrew pressed her against one of the barn's walls and did what he'd been aching to do for three long days now. He kissed the hell out of Layla Matthews.

CHAPTER 12

TO Roxxy, it felt like Andrew was doing nothing less than reaching inside of her and kissing her down to her very soul. This kiss stripped her of every ounce of cool she'd carefully cultivated over the years and turned her into the clueless teenager she'd been before the clothes and makeup and the voice coaches and PR agents.

Andrew's kiss made her feel awkward, like she wanted something from him, wanted it so much, but didn't know how to go about getting it.

She fumbled badly with the snap buttons of his Western shirt, only to have him tear it open with one yank and then pull her t-shirt over her head and undo her bra so quickly, she wondered if he'd laid out an action plan for how he was going to strip her naked before he came out to barn.

"It can't be like when we were in college," he said, covering her neck with kisses. "I can't give you time or wait for you to be comfortable with us like I did last time. Oh God, Layla, I want to fuck you so bad. I want to feel your naked pussy all over my cock..."

He unbuttoned her pants. And suddenly his long dick was nestled inside her panties, rubbing against her wet folds and making it so she didn't know if the liquid she was feeling between them was his pre-cum or her own raging need.

"Please tell me you're on birth control."

Finally something she didn't have to lie about. "I am," she said, silently thanking her mother for convincing her to get an IUD to help with her heavy periods when she turned twenty-five.

He kissed her hard and long again, his cock rubbing

into her pussy so deliciously, she was afraid she'd humiliate herself by coming all over it again. "Invite me in," he said against her lips.

"What?" she asked.

"I want an invitation. I want you to understand that you, Layla Matthews, are inviting me, Andrew Sinclair, to fuck you but good."

Again, Roxxy was not a virgin, but she might as well have been the way her cheeks warmed under this command. "Please have sex with me, Andrew. You're invited in."

He stroked the side of her face with his knuckles. "You're lucky I'm so hot for you right now," he said with grave seriousness. "Next time I'm going to make you ask a hell of a lot nicer than that."

Before she could question what "nicer" would entail, he was inside her. And then he was pounding her wet pussy so hard with one hand pressed into her clit, she felt her eyes roll backwards.

And the feelings! They were so intense, she couldn't hold on for long. "Oh God, Andrew! I'm coming."

"No, stay with me," he said, removing his hand and slowing down, so he was rolling up into her, thrusting into her hard, but without enough clitoral stimulation for her to come.

"I want you feel this with me," he said against her ear. "Feel how hard my cock is inside your pussy. Feel how bad I want you? I want you to feel it."

She definitely felt it. It was like he had her filled up so perfectly, if he wanted to spend the next fifty years cruising inside her like this, she'd die knowing she'd lived a life of total bliss.

Or at least she thought she wouldn't mind a slower pace. But soon her body made it clear it needed more from

Andrew, more than even this.

"Andrew, please," she said. "I need you. I need you to really fuck me. I'm so close."

This seemed to galvanize him. The lazy cowboy disappeared and soon he was pounding into her again with double the force of the first time. All it took was for him to dig two fingers into the folds of her pussy and she exploded, so bright and loud, she pushed him over the edge too.

He let out a keening sigh, then released inside her, flooding her with his seed. Only when he seemed to be completely empty did he stop moving. He fell against her, his body heavy and satisfied.

"Sweetheart, I don't think we're going to make it all the way back to the house tonight," he said with a lopsided smile.

Lying curled up on four hay bales with Andrew shouldn't have made for the most comfortable night of sleep she'd had in Montana so far, but somehow it did. Her dreams weren't plagued by strange images. In fact, she didn't dream at all, just slept more peacefully then she had in years, curled up in Andrew's arms.

And she would have stayed like that for hours more, except they were awakened at what felt like the crack of dawn by a heavy pounding on the door.

They both came awake with a start. But while Roxxy was still trying to push through the fog to figure out what was going on, Andrew was already shoving her clothes at her.

"Put these on," he mumbled. Then he pulled on his own jeans and cracked open the barn door.

"Sorry to bother you, boss," she heard one of the ranch hands say.

Before he could finish, a pot-bellied man pushed past

the hand and came storming into the barn.

"What's this all about, Joe?" Andrew asked.

"You're not dating my daughter anymore, Sinclair. You can call me Sheriff Thompson."

He eyed Roxxy, who had just managed to get her shirt on, with obvious contempt. "So this is who you dumped her for?"

Andrew folded his arms. "I'm assuming you wouldn't be on my ranch, in my town, unless you had a good reason, so I suggest you start talking now."

"Well, we just found a dead body at the Ride 'Em Cowboy Motel with a phone, a phone it seems you've called several times in the past few days." Sherriff Thompson seemed almost gleeful when he said, "So I'm going to need you to come with me back to the station and answer some questions."

CHAPTER 13

"**GUESS** what I'm doing right now," said the D.A. in lieu of a hello when he got on the phone. "I'm putting your name on a list. It's a very special list, I've labeled, 'The List of Idiots Who Are Obviously Looking to Get Killed Because They Refuse to Follow Instructions.'"

Roxxy pursed her lips. After her last scolding, it had taken her a while to drum up the nerve to call the D.A.'s office again, especially from the landline in her room. But she couldn't shake the feeling that the dead body at the motel had something to do with Mr. Kass. "I wouldn't be calling if it wasn't important."

"Let me guess, your host forgot to include lumps of sugar with the tea service," the D.A. said.

"No, sir, it really is important this time. My host just got arrested by the Buellton sheriff in connection with a dead body they found at the Ride 'Em Cowboy Motel. I'm afraid the body might belong to Mr. Kass."

The D.A. cursed. "Hold on."

He put her on hold for a long time, over thirty minutes, but Roxxy stayed on the line. She was too anxious to let a long wait keep her from finding out what was going on. Still, she was almost ready to hang up and try calling back, when the D.A. abruptly came back on the line.

"Unfortunately, it looks like it was our guy," he said, his voice considerably more grim than when he'd first answered the phone. "And we're thinking he might have been poisoned. The local police found two cups of tea next to the microwave. But it was a brand we'd never heard of before, couldn't even find it online. Something called 'Ras Jonny's Special Mix.' Sound familiar?"

Roxxy gasped. "That's the special tea Dexter makes

for me. He gets it from a Jamaican herbalist in the Bronx where he lives."

"So you think Dexter gave him the tea, maybe intending it for you to drink it? Or the both of you?"

Roxxy did remember overhearing Dex tell Mr. Kass that under no circumstance should she made to drink alone, but…"No! Dexter is my friend. One of my few true friends, he'd never—"

"I don't have the stats in front of me, but do you know how many stalking cases end up being completely anonymous. Very few. Usually it's somebody close to the victim. Think about it. How much do you really know about this Dexter?"

She did think about it, and unfortunately she didn't come up with much. She knew Dex was gay, but other than that, he was notoriously close-lipped about his private life, which he couldn't have much of since he made himself available twenty-four-seven to act as her one-man security force.

The few questions he had answered had been met with monosyllabic answers, until she'd backed off, figuring it was impolite to pry.

"Okay, I don't know much about him," she admitted. "But he passed a background check to get the job. And I think after this many years, I'd know his heart. He would never hurt anyone."

"You're telling me your ex-Special Forces bodyguard who gets paid to beat down anyone who even dares to touch you would never hurt anyone?"

"Not without reason," she insisted, but her resolve was weakening. She thought she knew Dexter, but she'd been burned enough times in the music business to know it wasn't wise to put complete faith in anybody—not even yourself. Still…"Why now? Why would he do this?"

"You had just come off a tour. Did he have any reason to believe you might be firing him any time soon?"

Roxxy gripped the phone. "Actually, I was planning to go back to school full time in the fall. He was the only one who knew about it."

"Mmm-hmm..." the D.A. answered in a tone that conveyed he had seen it all and was now incapable of surprise. "I'm going to send a few units to pick up your friend in the Bronx or wherever he's holed up. I think we might be closing this case sooner than later."

Despite what Dexter might have done, Roxxy's heart ached for him. "Maybe I could talk to him when you bring him in. He doesn't like to talk to people, but maybe he'll talk to me or at least tell me why he did this."

"You realize if Steve Kass hadn't gotten you out of the city, this guy would have already killed you by now, right?" the D.A. asked her.

"Yes, but—"

"Yes, but nothing. He's murdered one of mine, so here's how this thing's going to go down. We're going to pick up Dexter. Your host will be released from the county jail, but when he gets back, you're going to act like you don't know word one about this case until we come and get you.

"Wait, you want me to keep on lying to him?" Roxxy asked. "Why?"

"We've learned the hard way that it's best to keep a witness in protection until we've got the suspect firmly in hand. But don't worry, it's not some mafia guy who can put a hit on you from jail, so this should only take a few more days. Soon we'll come get you, and you'll be able to return to your old life, stalker-free."

He hung up then, apparently considering the conversation finished, but Roxxy didn't replace the phone in the cradle for a long time.

Funny, but her old life didn't sound that appealing anymore. In fact, the only thing less appealing was continuing to lie to Andrew for however long it took until the D.A.'s office came to retrieve her.

ANDREW DIDN'T QUITE KNOW WHAT to make of what had happened to him that day. First, he'd been brought back to the police station in Buellton by his ex-girlfriend's father. He'd figured out from the sheriff's questions alone that the man at the motel must have been Steve, who he'd been trying to get in contact with for over three days now with no return calls, but the sheriff and his deputies had been downright reluctant to believe his tale of a friend in New York who had asked him to hide some sort of unnamed informant at his ranch.

"So you're trying to say somebody from the New York mob came all the way to Montana to poison your friend and do God knows what with the witness and then left the body in the hotel to decay so bad, the manager came in because he was getting complaints about the smell?"

Andrew made a mental note to check in with Ray Bob, the manager/owner of the motel. Even though he'd bought Sinclair Township, Ray Bob owned the motel and could technically run it however he pleased. Still, it didn't look good for a motel in his township to only have as-needed maid service. Andrew suspected quite a few of Buellton's transits and meth heads were taking advantage of the motel's low weekly rates and "no questions asked" policies.

"I'm not trying to tell you anything," Andrew said to the sheriff. "I'm telling you exactly what happened. Were there any other numbers on the phone in the room? Ones

The Wild One

with New York area codes?"

From the looks a few of the deputies exchanged behind the sheriff's back, Andrew could tell he'd guessed something right.

But the sheriff stubbornly set his jaw. "So you think there's a second dead body we haven't found yet. You want to tell us about that one, too? Maybe you can lead us to it."

Andrew shook his head and raised his hands. "With all due respect, sir, I'm done answering questions until you at least call Steve's office in New York to corroborate my story."

The sheriff didn't move a finger to make any such call, just asked him question after increasingly insulting question, all of which Andrew answered with respectful silence.

Finally the phone rang, interrupting the one-sided interrogation. A deputy answered it and his eyes widened in surprise. "Hold on a minute," Andrew heard the young man say.

The deputy then pulled the sheriff aside and said something to him in a low voice, something that caused an angry look to come over his face. "Throw him in a cell while I take care of this," the sheriff said.

And that's how Andrew ended up spending most of the day in a jail cell, the nice guy slowly fuming out of him the longer he was made to wait.

By the time a deputy came to release him, it was dinner time and the sun was sitting low in the Montana sky.

"I suggest you keep your nose clean from now on, Mr. Sinclair," the sheriff said as a deputy handed him back a bag holding his personal items. "You may own that town of yours, but remember, I've still got jurisdiction there, and I'll be watching you. If you so much as speed, we'll be hauling you into that cell again. Might put a plaque on it just like the one you have on that little ranch of yours. We'll call it something hoity toity, like the 'The Sinclair Cell and Resort.'"

The sheriff seemed to like the laugh that bon mot got from his deputies, because he went on. "Maybe we'll catch that little black girl of yours up to something and have her spend a night or two with us, too. If she wants, she can wear that mini skirt we heard she was parading around in for a few days. Give the deputies something to look at it."

Two of the deputies snickered.

Andrew didn't allow his face to show emotion at all, but his voice became dangerous and low. "I'm a nice guy. I like to keep my business drama-free and I try to treat everybody I encounter fair and square. You're upset because I hurt your daughter. I understand, so I'm going to let this slide. Once. But understand something, you will never bring me in here again. Even if you find me at a crime scene covered in blood, you will question me in my home and at my leisure. And if I find out one of your deputies so much as says a single wrong word to Layla, then you're going to find yourself without a job. I don't care how well we used to get along."

He then pointed his first two fingers at the deputies who had snickered at the sheriff's threat against Layla. "But you two, I don't owe anything, so you can go ahead and pack up your personal belongings. You no longer have jobs on the Buellton police force."

The sheriff's face went blotchy with anger, "Where do you think you get off? You're not in the big city anymore and you don't have any jurisdiction over me."

Andrew picked up his smart phone and went into his contact list. "That's what weird about small towns. They always think they're so different from big cities, when it fact they're even worse." He pushed a button on his speed dial. "For example if I were still living in a big city like Pittsburgh—which by way is only mid-sized—I might have to make two calls to get you and your whole department fired, but here, my life is much easier—"

He broke off and smiled into the phone. "Hello, sir. I hope you don't mind me interrupting your dinner. Unfortunately, I've been in a jail cell at the Buellton police department since early this morning. Isn't this department run by someone you endorsed in his last election?" He gave the sheriff a significant look. "And I believe a few of our mutual friends gave him substantial campaign contributions."

He then listened for a few moments, before saying, "Sure, I'll put him on the phone. Nice talking to you, sir. Sorry about interrupting your dinner. No, I don't have time to come over tonight to join you guys. I wish I did, because I'm still remembering those smothered pork chops from the last time…they were worth the three hour drive. Rain check."

He handed the phone over to the sheriff and said sotto voce, "It's the governor for you. Apparently, he didn't want to hear what I was arrested for, he just wants to talk to you."

The sheriff answered the phone with a stammering, "Y-y-yes, sir? I understand sir. No, I've already indentified the deputies responsible for the oversight and have given them their walking papers. Yes, sir. No, I promise you it will never happen again, sir."

One of the deputies, who hadn't laughed at the sheriff's threat against Layla, ended up driving him home. But Andrew couldn't get Steve out of his mind. The man had had been an oily prick who only cared about his career, but he had gotten a lot of bad guys off the street and he didn't deserve to die like this.

He pulled out his phone and made a note to send his family flowers the next time he was at a computer. But before he could finish thumbing in the reminder, the phone lit up with his brother's name.

Andrew's heart went cold in his chest. Nathan was finally calling him back. Probably about Layla. He clicked a side button and sent the call to voicemail, then immediately deleted the message that popped up on his voicemail list soon after.

So much for Mr. Nice Guy. Layla was his now, he thought, his mind flashing back to how responsive she'd been to his every touch the night before. He wasn't about to give her back to Nathan.

"Can you drive faster?" he asked the deputy, suddenly more anxious than ever to get back to Layla and lose himself in her sweet curves.

But when he got home, he found the house dark and empty, with Layla nowhere to be found.

CHAPTER 14

ROXXY had been all over the world, but she'd never seen anything as drop dead gorgeous as the Montana night sky. She sat in a little meadow, about a mile down the creek from Sinclair Ranch, looking up at that sky, mesmerized by its beauty and wishing on its stars. As if they could make it so her most trusted friend hadn't just been exposed as a crazed stalker, as if they could get her out of this mess with Andrew.

The main object of many of her thoughts, Andrew, chose that moment to come loping into the meadow, with the lazy grace of a tiger. But something burned in his eyes that told her he was only half-joking when he tipped his hat toward her and said, "I see you've found a new place to hide from me."

She smiled, treating it like a joke, as if that hadn't been exactly what she was doing. "But, alas, you found me."

"After looking in the barn, and just about everywhere else. One of the hands said they'd seen you headed toward the river. Hard to keep secrets in this place." He sat down next to her.

Not as hard as you think, she thought. But out loud she said, "I don't get many chances to be this close to nature, and when I do, it's usually a beach at a secluded resort."

He nodded. "Nathan and his beach vacations. I bet you couldn't pay him to rough it out here."

"I don't think you could pay most people to come to Montana if white sandy beaches were on the table." She looked back up at the stars. "But they don't know what they're missing."

"That's how I felt when I first came here," he said. "But I'm surprised you feel the same way. I could barely get you to take hikes with me back when we were dating in Pittsburgh."

"A hike in Pittsburgh and a hike out here are two different things entirely," she said. "Montana, it's like nothing I've ever seen before. Just looking at the sky for a minute or two makes me feel like everything's going to be okay, like my problems really aren't as big as I think they are, not as big as that sky at least."

Andrew nodded. "I thought I came back here to get away after you married Nathan. But when I moved to Montana for good, it felt like I had finally found the place where I belonged. Now you're back and the picture's complete."

A wave of guilt washed over her. "Andrew…"

"Don't say anything," he said, his voice taking on a certain hard edge. "We don't have to talk about feelings yet." He stood up and held out his hand. "Let's go back to the house."

So that was what they did, in silence, both seemingly lost in faraway thoughts. When they entered the house and Andrew took off his cowboy hat, she had to resist the urge to run her hand through his sun-kissed hair. *He's not yours*, she reminded herself. *Not really.*

They walked up the stairs, and she stopped outside the door to her bedroom. "Well, thanks for coming to get me. I don't know if I would have been able to find my way back in the dark without you." She gave him what she hoped was a decent semblance of a light smile. "Good night."

But before she could turn the doorknob, his hand was on top of hers. "I've had a long day, so I'm going to cut straight to the point. From now on, you're sleeping in my bed."

"I think it's better if I sleep in my own." She tried to keep her voice firm as she said this, but she could hear it shaking.

He sighed. "You're pissing me off with this, Layla."

"I'm not trying to," she said. "It's just, like you were saying he other day, I've changed. A lot. I'm not the Layla you used to know, and I don't want to disappoint you. I've disappointed a lot of people in my life, and I don't want to disappoint you, too."

"Nathan's an asshole."

She shook her head. "Andrew..."

"No, I'm serious, if he let you go, if he made you feel like you were a disappointment, then he's an asshole." He took her hand off the doorknob. "Now come to bed with me where you belong."

Where you belong. She let him pull her along, her conscience telling her one thing, but her heart making it seem as if she really didn't have a choice. He was the first man, the only man, she'd ever been comfortable enough to have sex with stone cold sober. That alone made him irresistible, not to mention the fact that last night's coming together had been spectacular, better than the stars in the Montana sky even.

She wanted nothing more than to share Andrew's bed as much as she could, as many times as she could, until the D.A.'s office came to get her. And there was no excuse she could give to Andrew that would explain not doing exactly what they both wanted, without also blowing her cover.

When they got back to his room, he didn't waste much time. He once again pulled her t-shirt over her head and unhooked her bra. Then he pushed his face into hers, rubbing his five-o-clock shadow against her smooth cheek, which sent a weird thrill through her body, all the way down to her core.

"Pants," he said, as if sensing the flurry of activity he

was causing down there.

She quickly dispensed of her pants and hiking boots, only to have him nudge her back onto bed.

She had a slight moment of panic when she ended up splayed out in front of him on her back, but he didn't try to lie on top of her like the last time he had her on her back. Instead he stayed standing and oh-so-slowly pulled her cotton panties off.

For a moment he stared at her naked pussy. "I never would have expected you to keep it hairless like this. That just doesn't say Layla to me."

"Surprise," she tried to joke, but it sounded weak, since she was growing increasingly self-conscious under his stare. She'd gone through a leotard phase in her career, and getting permanent laser hair removal, even for her lady parts had just made sense. Who knew Andrew would find it so attractive?

"I've been thinking about getting a good look at it all day. About tasting you like this…"

He dropped his head down and dipped his tongue in. She nearly bucked off the bed. The problem with drunken sex was it usually didn't inspire oral on the guy's part and when it did, it tended to be sloppy.

But the way Andrew kissed her down there, it was like his tongue had a strange electricity in it, and it shot bolts of desire down both her thighs to the point that she could feel herself creaming into his mouth.

"I love how wet you get for me, are you going to stay this wet when I have my dick all the way inside you?"

She moaned.

"I'll take that as a yes," he said. Then he moved his tongue from her clit to the entrance of her tunnel, using his nose to maintain pressure on the button he was no longer lathing. It shouldn't have felt as good as having his cock inside her, but then he started swirling his tongue around her opening, using his thumb to rub her clit and like a tenacious explorer, he found her G-spot. She came apart and to her embarrassment, actually squirted into his mouth. But she was coming too hard. She couldn't breathe, much less squeeze words out for an apology.

Andrew laughed. "If you're going to make me swallow, you're going to have to return the favor soon."

But before she could answer that, he said. "Turn over. I want to get a look at the sweet ass you were barely hiding under that skirt."

She did as he said, glad he didn't want to go for missionary, which would have made her freak out no matter how turned on she was.

"I like this picture," she heard him say behind her. She could practically feel his eyes devouring her. "Do me a favor and fuck my hand. My thumb's already had it's fun, now I want my whole hand to smell like you."

Her breath caught as he eased his first two fingers into her then paused, honestly expecting her to do as he said.

Roxxy's mind had reservations, but her body seemed to have no problems with the command whatsoever. She felt herself moving back and forth on his fingers, only stopping with a gasp when he added in the third.

"I wasn't sure if I'd be able to get four fingers into you. You were tight last night. But you're so wet right now, I think we ought to try. Open wider for me, sweetheart."

This time there was no hesitation, like the wanton woman she'd thought she had only been pretending to be on stage, she greedily opened her legs for the fourth finger, crying out with pleasure as she rocked her hips back and forth on his hand, which was now covered with her essence.

She was acting like a total slut, but she didn't care. She

was so close to coming again, all she cared about was making it over that edge. And then the fingers were gone, and she whimpered.

"Sorry," she heard him say. And then came the sound of him unzipping his jeans. "You're too fucking hot to toy with for too long. My cock is threatening mutiny if I don't let it inside of you. But I need an invitation."

"You're invited!" she assured him. "Please put it inside of me, now. Please."

Despite his insinuation the night before that he would make her beg the next time, he pushed inside of her without further delay and she nearly collapsed on the bed, the pleasure of having him fill her was so intense. His hand had been good, but having him come at her from behind, she'd never felt anything like it. It wasn't long before she felt her pussy clamping down on his cock, sucking him into her own orgasm. She came first, but he toppled soon afterwards, squeezing his fingers into her hips, like vices, until his own cum was fully released inside of her.

He fell into the bed beside her, breathing hard. They didn't say a thing, just let the afterglow slide over them, until their breathing evened out.

Andrew wrapped his arms around her from behind, just like he had in the barn, and for a minute she thought maybe he had fallen asleep. But then he whispered into her ear, "I don't know what was going on with you tonight, but if you go back to him, I'll never fucking talk to you again. I won't be able to be chivalrous next time."

"I won't," she said, meaning it. Because she didn't care who this Nathan was, she couldn't imagine he had anything on his brother.

"But if you do…"

"I won't," she said again.

He seemed to accept this, because pretty soon he really did fall asleep. And she did, too.

CHAPTER 15

THIS time it wasn't knocking that woke her from her delicious sleep but a certain grinding. More specifically, Andrew behind her, moving his hips in a circle, with his bold erection lodged against the bottom of her now panty-clad pussy.

Late last night she'd gotten up to use the bathroom and had gone back to her room to retrieve a new pair of underwear and a t-shirt. But now she was regretting her late night concession to modesty, because it was getting in the way of her morning delight.

Was he asleep? She kind of liked the idea of him losing control of himself and spilling all over her panties, the way she'd done all over him.

But soon he dashed that small hope. "You covered up," he growled in her ear.

"I'm really wishing I hadn't," she confessed, pushing back against him so she could feel more of his hard length against her slit.

At the same time, his arms snaked under her top, and he took hold of her breasts, pressing the globes together in a way that made her squirm so bad against him, it felt like her pussy was on fire.

"Fuck, Layla," he said in her ear. "Give me an invitation."

"You're invited," she told him. "Get in."

"No, even nicer than that."

"Get in, please."

He chuckled behind her. "Even nicer. I know you can be very nice if you put your mind to it."

For a few moments, Roxxy's brain reeled. What did he mean? How could she ask any nicer?

In a fit of desperation, she reached down and pulled aside the crotch of her panties, revealing the naked pussy Andrew loved so much, now slick with her juices. "See how bad I want you, Andrew?" she said. "Please come in."

"Fucking hell, Layla." His hands went from her breasts to her shoulders, hooking over them and pulling her down so her wet pussy slid onto his hard cock without any further conversation.

"Oh, sweetheart, you're so tight and wet," he said. "How long do you think you'll last this time before coming all over my cock again?"

She honestly didn't know, and she was too overcome by the way he was thrusting up into her to even attempt to answer. He was packed so tight into her pussy, she could feel the pulse of his cock as he moved inside her.

It got to the point that she had to bite down on one of the hands he had on her shoulder to keep from screaming.

But he didn't let her go, just kept thrusting into her hard and long, his strong arms squeezing her swollen breasts together, the cool air of the overhead fan making her shiver. Her exposed front side was now covered with sweat, and she could feel her naked pussy quivering, begging for even more.

As if reading her mind, he said. "You're still with me. Is it because you're one of those girls who needs to be released?"

Her clit responding with a throbbing scream. "Yes! Yes!" she said. "Please, touch me there."

Andrew made a tutting sound. "My hands are too busy keeping you on my cock. You're going to have to touch yourself for me, sweetheart. I've jerked off enough thinking about you. Let me see how you look touching yourself with me inside you."

Her manic clit didn't let her have any modesty, even on

this point. She reached down and started working two fingers against her swollen button. The other one came up to her breasts and began to rub the nipple.

He grunted out, almost like he was in pain, and she felt him bury his face in the back of her neck. "I was wrong. I can't watch you do that or I'm going to lose it."

"It's okay if you lose it," she told him. Then her swollen pussy lips clenched around her fingers and the other hand tightened over her nipple as she showed him exactly what she meant by losing it.

"Oh, Andrew!" She went rigid, then she shuddered to a conclusion, every body part tingling with amazing sensation. It felt like her heart had burst open and released confetti.

And throughout it all, Andrew held her close, as if her coming gave him more pleasure than his own release, which she distantly noted still hadn't happened.

"Sweetheat, that was so fucking hot," he said, coming out of her. "Turn over. I want to see you right now."

She turned over and was taken aback by the softness in his eyes, like he was in awe of having her there, in his bed. But not because she was a worldwide celebrity, just because she was a woman and he wanted her.

He looked at her for so long, she began to think that was how he would spend the morning, despite the lingering evidence of his continued arousal. But then he cupped her around the back of her neck and captured her mouth in a slow kiss that burned all the way down to her womb.

She had sung about these kinds of kisses before, but never had she received one quite like this. The way Andrew explored her mouth with his, it wasn't like anything she'd ever felt before. And soon she was feeling hot and bothered below, becoming newly desperate to have him inside her again.

"You didn't come," she said against his mouth. "Do you need another invitation? Because believe me, the last one still stands."

He laughed against her lips. "Don't worry, sweetheart. I intend to take full advantage of your beautiful body, but I'm going to take my time."

He slipped inside of her, and began slowly rolling his hips into her. "No rushing me. If it takes all morning, it takes all morning."

Feeling bold, she asked, "But how about if my clit needs extra attention again? After all, I am one of those girls."

"No more touching yourself either," he said, with a smile. "Tell your clit not to worry. I'll take care of it." He kissed her again. "When I'm ready to."

As if to illustrate his point, his rolling strokes became so slow that by the time each one was done, nothing inside her pussy had been left untouched, including her clit.

She closed her eyes, wondering how she could become so hot for him again after just having the best orgasm of her life. Later she would regret this action, closing her eyes and letting him completely take over. If she'd kept them open and if she hadn't been so sex drunk, she might have been able to stop him before he did what he did next.

But as it was, he caught her completely by surprise when he flipped her over onto her back.

One minute she was feeling like the most cherished woman in the world, and the next, she was sixteen again, with a sweaty record label head lying on top her, using his weight and muscle to pin her down beneath him.

"No! No!" she screamed.

"What? Now, you want to act like you didn't know what this meeting was all about?" the exec asked. "You think the head of a major music label is just going to invite you up to his office after everybody else has gone home because he really wants to hear you audition?"

That was exactly what she had thought, exactly what her mother had told her this meeting would be about. She just had to sing a couple of songs for him a capella, Shirelle had said, prove she had true talent, and that her demo hadn't been a fluke.

She hadn't been prepared when the executive had invited her to sit down on his leather couch and then unexpectedly took a seat right beside her, uncomfortably close. But she didn't want to disappoint Shirelle, who had told her they needed this contract to finally make their dreams come true.

"Be nice," she'd told Roxxy, who was known to clam up or withdraw when she got too nervous. "Keep on smiling and talking to him. I don't care how nervous you are."

So that was what she did when the exec sat so close to her, the sides of their legs were touching. She even managed to keep her smile pasted on when he put a clammy hand on her bare knee.

But when he'd started kissing her, and pushed her back into the couch, she couldn't pretend anymore, even after he chastised her for not knowing the deal from the beginning.

"No! No!" she screamed again when he grabbed the hands that were trying to push him off and pinned them above her head.

But it was too late. He'd gotten underneath the short school skirt she was wearing and ripped into her, tearing into her hymen without another thought.

"Get off me! Get off me!" Hot tears of pain and frustration filled her eyes, and she bucked her hips, trying to dislodge him, even though she could barely move under his heavy weight.

Somehow she managed to work one hand free and scratch his face, so hard it left tracks of blood.

In the original version, he'd screeched, then raised up and punched her in the face, once, twice, three times, so she could do little more than loll her head to the side in a daze as he finished on top of her, seemingly even more turned on by the fact that her face was now a bloody mess. It'd taken weeks for her face to heal, but her mother had been overcome with glee. Apparently this had been much better than her suggestion of being nice to the label head, because he'd agreed to a two-record deal to avoid Shirelle pressing charges on her daughter's behalf.

But in this new version, after Roxxy scratched him, she felt his weight lift off of her. Suddenly she was free to move, and when she came back to herself...

...There was Andrew, holding his face, which she'd scratched bloody, and looking at her like she was an alien.

"I'm sorry," she croaked, barely able to get the words past the lump in her throat. "I didn't mean to—"

She couldn't finish the sentence. Instead, she scrambled out of bed and ran out of the room and into her own, locking the door behind her.

It took a good, long time curled up in a fetal ball with her back to the door for her to calm down enough to crawl into bed. And even after she did, she continued crying so hard, she thought she might choke on her own tears.

Why couldn't she just be normal? Like the real Layla? Like every other woman in the world who could handle something as mundane as the missionary position—especially after having the orgasm of her life with the sexiest man she had ever known.

She fell asleep sobbing and wishing she were anyone

under the sun but her own miserable self.

CHAPTER 16

PART of what made Andrew a natural born leader was, unlike his brother, he knew how to talk to people and was good at figuring out solutions all parties involved could work with. That's why he'd been appointed the head of Global Initiatives at Sinclair Industries, and that's why he'd been able to put a nearly bankrupt dude ranch into the black in under a year, not to mention gather enough capital to buy the town it was housed in.

That afternoon, he met with the owner of the Ride 'Em Cowboy and presented him with plans to renovate the motel in ways that just might help everyone forget a dead body had been found there less than a day ago. He set rolling grand opening dates for five new guest ranches. And he even got through a bit of the paperwork for the camp he was planning for underprivileged kids.

However, Andrew "Big Idea" Sinclair had no idea how to handle the ex-girlfriend who had unexpectedly come back into his life. It was so bad that when his phone had erupted later in the afternoon with another call from Nathan, he'd been tempted to answer it, if only to question his brother about what had happened to Layla.

But then he'd sent the call to voicemail at the last minute, thinking about that morning. When he'd gone to her door and heard her ragged crying on the other side, like her heart was breaking, he'd wanted nothing more than to gather her up in his arms and reassure her everything would be all right.

But it was more than obvious the last thing she needed was any more attention from him. He'd never had a girl freak out on him like that. For a moment, it had been hard to believe this was Layla he was dealing with. She had morphed into a crazed animal so quickly. One minute she had been begging him for more and the next, she'd scratched up his face.

He'd decided to let her cool off in her room. He ate breakfast and then went into his office to work. But when he came out, he found her door open and Layla gone from the house, as if she'd been waiting for him to turn his back just long enough for her to sneak out.

She didn't come home for lunch either, and when he tried to catch her at the staff table during dinner hours, he was told she'd already come through, grabbed some food, and left.

This was how he came to find himself waiting in the dark hay barn for a woman who obviously didn't want to see him. She came through the barn door just fifteen minutes after the bonfire ended, which meant she had come straight there, with no plans to attempt to face him back at the house.

In fact, she came to a stuttering stop when her flashlight landed on him standing next to the haystack where they'd slept two nights ago.

"Andrew!" she said.

"You sound more surprised to see me than I am to see you," he said.

She lowered the flashlight. "I thought it would be better if we spent tonight apart."

"Better for who?" he asked her. "Because I recollect telling you clearly last night you'd be sleeping in my bed from now on."

The moon wasn't very bright that night, so he couldn't see her expression in the dark barn. But he heard the way her voice trembled when she said, "I didn't think you'd want me there. After what happened this morning."

And his anger melted like a stick of butter. "Listen,

Layla," he said, coming to stand close to her, though he was careful not to touch her because it was obvious she was still pretty spooked. "Let me make this clear to you right now. I'll always want you in my bed. The only reason I didn't keep you there this morning was because you ran. Now, c'mon."

He resisted the urge to grab her hand. Andrew had been chasing after Layla for a long time, first in college, then right before she chose his brother over him, and now he'd been forced to all but hunt her down for the third night in the row. But at that moment, with the two of them standing there face to face, he knew it had to be her decision to step out of the dark barn with him.

He let out an inward sigh of relief when she took his hand and walked with him out to the dirt road that led back to his house.

But this time he only let about five minutes pass in silence before he said, "You swear to me Nathan didn't hurt you like that?"

She shook her head frantically. "No, this is something that happened a long time ago."

"Before you met me?" he asked.

"When I was sixteen." She kept her eyes on the dirt road in front of her.

"And that's the real reason you didn't want us to have sex when we were going out in college, because of what happened when you were sixteen?"

She looked away from him and mumbled. "Yeah, something like that. It's stupid and it was a long time ago. And as you saw before I went crazy on you, it doesn't have to be a big deal when it comes to sex, but missionary sort of triggers it, especially when a guy is lying on top of me."

"Has Nathan ever triggered it?"

She shook her head. "No. I've been pretty good at sticking with positions that are safe. I tell guys missionary's too boring for me, and they usually believe me. Most of them think it's kind of sexy."

Andrew's mouth thinned at the idea of other guys, especially ones like Nathan, too dim to see through Layla's act in bed. "I'm not most guys," he said.

"I know you aren't," she answered. "I've never lost control the way I did this morning, even when I've had too much to drink. Usually I don't even let myself close my eyes, because I know what will happen if a guy flips me on my back."

They arrived at the house then, and she waited until they'd walked up the steps of the wrap-around porch and Andrew had let them in before finishing with "I'm really sorry, Andrew."

"No," he said, suddenly pressing her into the nearest wall and claiming her lips with a kiss. "Don't apologize. Don't ever apologize to me again for that. It's not your fault. It's nobody's fault but the bastard who raped you when you were sixteen. I don't suppose you want to tell me his name."

She shook her head sadly. "It wouldn't matter if I did. He died of cancer two years ago, so it's too late for any kind of revenge."

Andrew went quiet at that reveal. Disappointment coursed through him. At that moment he wanted nothing more than to find the man who had done this to his Layla and beat him to a bloody pulp.

Misreading the look on his face, she laid a hand on his shoulder. "But please don't worry, okay? I'm not ever going to let myself freak out like that again. I'll make sure to keep my issues out of the bedroom from now on."

The look in her eyes was pleading with him to let the

uncomfortable subject drop, but he shook his head.

"No."

"No?" she said, confusion in her voice.

"No," he repeated. "I already told you. I'm not like most guys. I'm not going to force you to have sex with your eyes open all the time just to make sure I don't accidentally trigger you. And sweetheart, you drive me out of my mind with lust, so I can't guarantee I won't forget again."

"I don't understand," she said. "That's the only way I can have sex with any kind of guarantee I won't freak out. If you're trying to say that's not good enough for you…"

"I'm not trying to say that's not good enough for me. I'm telling you straight out plain it's not. I was in a dishonest marriage for years, I'm not going to start out with you like that."

"But we're not married."

He gave her a sharp look, but then decided not to say the word that immediately popped into his mind: "yet." It had been less than a week, and she was already spooked enough.

Instead he held out his hand to her again. "C'mon, sweetheart."

This time she took it without hesitation, but she did ask, "Where are we going?"

Andrew actually managed to smile at her despite the tension, thick in the air between them. "To bed."

CHAPTER 17

ROXXY had been through a lot over the last week: finding Mabel's body, discovering Dexter's betrayal, letting herself get triggered by Andrew. But somehow nothing that had happened to her so far seemed as scary as following Andrew up to his bedroom.

He was moving, yes, but in a way that reminded her of a marble statue, like he was made of resolve instead of flesh.

When they got to his room, she wasn't quite sure what to do with herself until he said, "Get naked and sit down on the bed."

So she did. Then to her consternation, he sat down right beside her.

"That day in the truck, you were nervous because I was sitting so close. This is how it started out with him, right?"

"Funny, I thought I did a pretty good job of covering up how nervous I was," she said.

He gave her that sad smile again. "No, it's not funny, Layla, and I need you to tell me what happened."

She swallowed, trying to get some moisture down her dry throat. "Yeah," she admitted. "He sat next me, just like you're doing. That's how it started. Then he put his hand on my knee."

To her surprise he placed his hand on her bare knee. "Like this? Whoa, sweetheart, relax," he said, when she seized up with fear. "We're going to sit here like this for a little while. I want you to look at my hand and realize it belongs to me, a man who cares deeply about you, not to your attacker."

She shook her head, unable to speak she was so frightened.

"Breathe," he said. "Breathe and say to yourself, 'that hand on my knee belongs to Andrew.' Say it out loud."

It took several tries, before she finally managed to squeeze out, "That hand on my knee belongs to Andrew." Several breaths then she tried it again. "That hand on my knee belongs to Andrew." More breaths, and another: "That hand on my knee belongs to Andrew."

She felt the muscles in her body begin to untighten a little. She kept staring at the hand on her knee, and it lost the four rings the executive had worn on his hammy fingers. Eventually, it morphed back into what it really was, Andrew's large hand with its long elegant fingers under which she could feel calluses from all the physical ranch work he insisted on doing, even though he had hired hands for that.

Soon her breathing calmed and she relaxed. At least she did until he said, "Now tell me what happened next."

"Then he, um…he, umm…kissed me. Not nice but ugly, just enough to take me by surprise, so he could get me under him."

"Like this." Andrew didn't waste time. He pressed his lips against hers and had her pinned under him in what felt like zero seconds flat.

And she completely freaked out.

"No! No!" she said, flashing back against her will.

Except this time when she tried to scratch him, he grabbed both her hands and pinned them above her head without having to be told that was what the music exec did. This caused her to freak out even more.

She screamed now, thrashing underneath his weight, trying with all her might to get away. It felt like she'd been dropped down a black hole, like the misery of that night was closing in on her. But then she heard a voice…

"Layla, Layla, it's me, Andrew. I need you to come

back. I need you to open your eyes and look at me now, so you can understand it's me on top of you, not that bastard who raped you."

She blinked, opening her tear-filled eyes to see the blurry image of Andrew. He was pinning her down, yes, but he was looking at her with such compassion, it was impossible to super-impose the label head's face on top of his.

"You know who I am, and you know I won't come inside you without an invitation," he told her. "We're going to just lie like this for however long you need it to be. I don't care if it takes all night. I can wait for my invitation."

She didn't believe him. Some animal part of her brain told her he'd either fuck her without permission or get sick of lying on top of her like this, and just give up on her.

But then an hour passed and they were still laid out in the weird tableau.

"My arms are starting to hurt," she said.

He brought them down, repositioning them between their bodies, so she was still pinned but no longer forced to lie with her arms above her head. If he was uncomfortable keeping her pinned but still making it so she didn't have to support all of his weight on top of her, he didn't say one word about it.

And soon another hour passed.

She was dry as a bone down there, and she was thinking it would take several more hours of silence before Andrew gave up on this venture of his, but then he said, "You know, I don't act the way I act with you with anybody else."

Her eyes widened with mock surprise. "You mean I'm the first girl you've pinned down like this?"

"Yes, and I also mean you're the first girl I've ever

cursed in front of, the first girl I've ever talked dirty to in any way. I was raised to be a gentleman, but you've probably noticed I have problems being a gentleman with you."

Roxxy shook her head. "If we're being honest, I had no idea you were raised to be anything close to a gentleman."

He gave her a wry smile. "You're wondering why I was so cold to you those first few days after you came to the ranch."

"I thought you were angry with me for coming here when you had a girlfriend."

"No, it was because you made my dick so hard, harder than any woman ever has before, just by looking at you. I was afraid to talk to you, much less spend any kind of time with you. I didn't think I'd be able to keep my hands off of you."

His eyes caressed her face. "You've probably been thinking all day that I'm turned off because of what some asshole did to you when you were sixteen. But I need you to understand something, sweetheart." His gray eyes met hers. "I could never not want you. I don't care if you used to be my brother's wife or what happened to us in the past. I wanted you from the day you came here to find me and I'll want you until the day I die. There is nothing that happened to you that could make me stop wanting you more than any other woman I've ever known or seen."

Tears filled her eyes again. She wished that were true. She wished she could keep him after the D.A.'s office came to get her and let him know who she really was.

"Close your eyes, sweetheart. Trust me."

She closed her eyes and soon found herself the recipient of the sweetest kiss she had ever known. It made no demands, and it took its own languorous time, as if to say Andrew would be perfectly happy kissing her for an eternity if she never saw fit to give him an invitation in this position.

The gentle kiss filled her heart, and wiped her mind clean of the music exec. Suddenly it was just her and Andrew, kissing on a cloud of desire.

She heard herself say, "You're invited in. I'm giving you an invitation."

And then his head was between her legs. He kept her arms pinned at her sides, but his mouth prepared her for his entrance in a way that let her know she was definitely dealing with Andrew Sinclair and not some asshole who liked to rape and beat up helpless teenagers.

Soon, she felt her eyes close again, and she became lost in the intimate kiss he was giving her private area, sucking on her clit and licking her pussy folds so hardcore, she didn't know if the new wetness inside her belonged to him or her. Probably both.

"Andrew, stop," she said. "Please fuck me. You have your invitation, now get inside of me."

This time when he pinned her arms above her head and settled on top of her, she didn't trigger. And when he began to move inside of her, riding her in an agreed upon rhythm with her hips, they both opened their eyes, each marveling at the beauty of the other, as he took them over the horizon into a sea of white light.

Only when they were both coming down from the orgasm did he let her arms go. They fell like puppet strings to her side as he rolled off of her, only to pull her over and place her head on his chest a few moments later.

"All right then," he said. "We can stick to the non-traumatic positions all you want, sweetheart. But the next time I accidentally trigger you, that's how we'll handle it, okay?"

"Okay," she agreed, feeling warm and fuzzy and safer

than she had ever believed she possibly could with a man. "Thank you," she said, meaning it from the bottom of her heart, and more than he would ever understand.

He kissed her on the top of her head. And her last thought before falling into contented sleep, was that Andrew must be lying, or at least exaggerating, about having never talked dirty to a woman before. He was so good at it, it didn't seem like it could possibly be true.

CHAPTER 18

WHEN Roxxy was a teenager, she read a tragic story featuring bowls of ice cream but no spoon. As someone who had been denied ice cream for years, she didn't quite get the moral of the tale back then, but over the next few days she came to understand it inside and out.

Being with Andrew Sinclair was nothing short of amazing, better than anything she had ever known, including the year she won five Grammys. True to his word, he had stuck to non-missionary positions and the sex only seemed to get better each time. It got to the point where they were going at it three times a day. In the morning, at night, and at least once a day Andrew found an excuse to pull her away from the children's program and have his way with her in whatever secluded nook they could find.

It got so bad that when he announced he had to go up the nearby mountain for a few days to oversee the renovations on Sinclair Chalet, the two-story ski lodge that attracted most of Sinclair Ranch's winter business, she came with him. She was so sprung, she even volunteered to sort out the non-profit paperwork for the camp, while she was there with him.

Andrew warned her non-profit paperwork was pretty complicated, but with him there to answer any questions she might have, she breezed through it. She ended up getting it all done by the Saturday before his trip. She even knocked out a rough draft of a presentation speech for the orgs he was meeting with in D.C. She presented it all to him in the lodge's great room, in front of the floor-to-ceiling windows, which led out to a view of the beautiful, snow-capped mountains just beyond.

Andrew, who had more heart than desire to deal with paperwork and speeches when it came to the non-profit aspects of his business, was thrilled with her work. "When I come back from the East Coast, let's talk about putting you in charge of the non-profit division of Sinclair Ranches."

"What?" she said, her eyes going wide.

"I was planning on hiring somebody anyway, and I can't see anybody doing a better job with this than you've done"

"But I don't have any experience. In fact, I was planning to go to the University of Southern California in the fall to get a degree in non-profit management so I could understand how to do this stuff better."

His eyes darkened. "So that was your plan. Lay low with me for the summer then disappear for college?"

"No," she answered. "I was originally planning to vacation for the rest of the summer and then go to college, but the...ah, divorce...kind of put a crimp in my original plans."

Andrew didn't answer, just went back to typing on his computer, leaving Roxxy to start incorporating the notes he'd given her on the extra laptop he'd dug up for her to work on.

But about thirty minutes later, he said, "Okay, I sent a note to a friend of mine on the board at University of Montana-Missoula. He says they don't have the same degree track as USC, but they offer a lot of the same courses, so you could technically cobble together your own degree program."

Again with the ice cream. "Andrew, I don't know..."

"Just think about it. You'd get on the ground experience running our camp program, and of course Sinclair Ranch would pay for your classes."

"You don't have to do that," she said.

"I want to do that. Do you know how hard it is to find somebody who not only wants to go the extra mile to get a children's camp off the ground, but also doesn't mind handling all the crazy non-profit paperwork—you are willing to handle any and all paperwork, right?"

"Yes, but—"

"It's a deal then."

He got out of his leather chair and pulled her into his arms.

"Wait, Andrew," she said, giggling. "I never agreed to anything."

"If you think I'm going to let you go to some other school far away from here and end up working for some West Coast non-profit, you're out of your mind," he said. His voice lowered and grew serious. "You're staying right here with me, sweetheart. I'm not taking no for an answer."

Roxxy didn't want to give him no for an answer. Who could say no to ice cream, even if you didn't have a spoon? "I'll think about it," she said.

He grinned down at her, large and wide, like he already knew he'd caught her in his trap. "You do that, sweetheart. And as long as I have you here, all soft and agreeable in my arms, lets talk about this interesting piece of lingerie I picked up in Buellton the other day."

Roxxy raised her eyebrows. "You did not buy lingerie for me."

"Peach lingerie to be exact. Bra that's only held together by a flimsy bow, panties with a sheer crotch. Very nasty stuff, none-too-befitting of a lady."

She grabbed him by the collar. "Good, because I'm not much of a lady. Especially when it comes to a gentleman like you..."

Less than an hour later, she was telling him, "I want you more than I want your brother." And then without warning, she heard herself say, "Andrew, I—I love you."

Roxxy gasped on the inside, not believing she'd let those words slip out of her mouth. She had known this man less than two weeks, and here she was declaring her love for him.

But then he gave her the most tender look and said, "It feels like I've been waiting my whole life to hear you say that. I love you too, sweetheart. So fucking much."

And then he showed her how much all afternoon long.

CHAPTER 19

WHEN they came down from the Sinclair Chalet that evening, Roxxy was sad to go. But Andrew's trip was the next day and he wanted to eat dinner with the staff at least once that week, since he wouldn't be back in town until the next Saturday.

"Maybe you should go without me," Roxxy said after they dropped off their luggage in Andrew's bedroom.

"I thought you hated eating alone."

"Yeah, but I should probably get over that, especially since you're going out of town." Plus, it seemed silly now, she thought to herself. She didn't care about staying as thin as possible anymore, and she'd already gained at least five pounds since coming here.

"What's wrong?" he asked. He came over to her and slipped his arms around her waist. "And before you say, 'nothing.' Remember, I don't like being lied to."

"Omission isn't exactly lying," she said.

"It's not being honest either. And I want you to be straight with me in all things."

Roxxy almost felt numb to the guilt at this point, it had become such a constant companion. And she once again wearily pushed it aside in order to answer his question. "The last time we saw your staff together we weren't dating. You were still with your perfect girlfriend, and they all thought you'd be asking her to marry you soon."

"You think they'll hold our relationship against us?"

"I think they'll think I stole another woman's man. I mean, that's what her father thought. That's probably what Amy thinks, too."

"But that's not what happened, and I doubt any of the staff will have the balls to say anything to you anyway. If they do, tell them truth. You didn't steal me from anybody. You had my heart as soon as you set foot in Montana. You can't steal what already belongs to you."

Roxxy's own heart melted. And not for the first time that week, she wished she could keep Andrew. More than anything, she wanted to be the woman he thought she was, to stay in his heart forever.

He was right about no one having the balls to say anything to her, though the reception definitely wasn't as warm as when she'd been Andrew's poor, recently divorced sister-in-law. At least Elena happily made room for the both of them at the table.

"We missed you at the children's program this week," she said.

"I missed you guys, too," Roxxy answered. "But hopefully we'll be able to get even more children up here with all the good work we got done at the ski lodge, planning the camp."

"So that's what you were doing up at the ski lodge all this time," Elena said. Her eyes twinkled with amusement. "Working."

"Among other things," Andrew said. He slipped an arm around Roxxy's shoulders in a move that felt like both a shield and a claim. "What have you all been up to since we were gone?"

A litany of work stories and small complaints ensued. The rest of the hour flew by with Andrew answering questions and letting them know what all he'd do about the handful of problems when he got back.

By the time dinner was through, a few of the staff members who hadn't greeted her at all when she sat down were asking her about the camp and what they were planning.

They just want Andrew to be happy, she realized as she

answered their enthusiastic questions. And she was struck with a sense of awe. There weren't many people in her life who cared about her happiness. One of them was dead, and the other had killed her. Again her heart ached for the loss of both friendships. She still was having a hard time believing that Dexter had done it, even with all the evidence pointing right at him.

"You okay?" Andrew asked her, jogging her out of her gloomy thoughts.

"Yeah," she answered. Another lie. She was just racking them up with him.

"You got quiet all of a sudden."

"I was just thinking. Sorry, did I miss something?"

Andrew nodded toward Elena on her other side. "Elena asked you a question."

"I was wondering if you and Andrew wanted to come out to The Palace. A bunch of us are going after the bonfire tonight."

"The Palace?"

"It's a honky tonk bar out on the Western edge of town," Andrew explained. "It's been there since the eighteen hundreds."

Roxxy might have given up her singing career, but the musician she used to be wouldn't let her pass up the opportunity to visit a music establishment that had been around for over two hundred years.

As it turned out, The Palace was an ironic name. The place was little more than a huge room with a stage and a bar. But the headshots and tour posters hanging on the wooden slat walls boasted an impressive array of chart-topping country musicians who had come through toward the beginning of their careers. And that night, Tennessee Big Shots, a band even she'd heard some buzz about, would be playing.

The Wild One

The jovial and longhaired owner, Walt, came out to greet Andrew less than five minutes after the Sinclair Ranch group walked in the door. From what she could glean from their conversation, Andrew had given him a very favorable lease deal after he'd bought the town, and for that, drinks were on Walt the entire night.

"My staff will appreciate it, but I've got to catch a plane in the morning, so I'm staying dry," Andrew yelled, over the country music flowing out of the juke box. "We're here because my lady wanted to see a real honky tonk with her own eyes."

Walt grimaced. "Unfortunately, the lead singer of Tennessee Big Shots is currently passed out in the backroom. Still breathing, but he must be on something because I can't wake him up to save my life."

Probably heroin, Roxxy thought. She'd never touched the stuff, but she knew plenty of musicians who'd ruined their careers early on it.

"So unless I can find another singer, no live music tonight."

"Layla can sing," Elena said. "Really well."

"You can?" both Andrew and Walt asked.

"Um ... well," she hedged. This was hitting a little too close to home.

"She can," Elena assured them. "She often sings to the children at the end of the day. They don't want her to stop, her voice is so pretty."

Andrew grinned at her. "Well, you said you liked country western music. Here's your chance to prove it."

"But I'm no professional country and western singer," she said.

"That don't matter," Walt said. "Most nights people are satisfied with a warm body. If you can cover a few songs, the rest of Tennessee Big Shots can back you up."

"I only know five, maybe six country songs by heart."

"That's enough for me. Get up there and when you're done with those five songs, just go through them again. I'll offer some drink specials at the bar. People won't notice if they're drunk enough."

And that's how Roxxanne Weathers found herself on a stage less than two weeks after vowing never to step foot on one again.

"What the hell," one guy said when she took the stage. "That ain't Tennessee Big Shots. That's some black girl."

"Shut up and let her sing," one of the Sinclair staff members shouted back.

Then Andrew led a chant of "Layla! Layla! Layla!" which was soon taken up by at least half the club.

Roxxy hadn't performed in a venue this small – well, ever. But somehow it made her more nervous than performing in front of a stadium filled with people.

She tentatively started into one of her favorite Colin Fairgood songs, and to her surprise, people soon started clapping along. A few people even started dancing.

After that, she did three more of Colin's few upbeat songs, and then she launched into some of her crossover favorites, like Dolly Parton's "9 to 5" and Kenny Rogers "The Gambler" and songs by Loretta Lynn, Sugarland, Little Big Town, and Darius Rucker.

When she'd exhausted her supply of upbeat country songs, she did a quick consult with the band, and they cobbled together "fiddle" versions of the few pop hits they all knew.

The joint went crazy when she launched into a country-fried version of "Crazy in Love" by Beyonce. And by the time she got to the last song in her pop/county set, a version of "Wild Ones," edited down to only the parts that had originally been sung by Sia, it seemed everyone in the

The Wild One

club was dancing. She even saw Walt twirling Elena around on the floor.

The only one who wasn't dancing was Andrew, who stood right where he had from the beginning, at the edge of the stage, watching Roxxy with such pride in his eyes.

And suddenly Roxxy didn't feel much like singing anymore. "I've had a lot of fun with you guys tonight, but this is going to be my last song."

The crowd booed at this announcement.

"No, booing, no booing," she said to them with a laugh. "Don't make this sad, because honestly, this has been the best day of my entire life. I want you to grab your sweetheart close and really feel the words I'm singing with this next song."

The band then launched into her favorite country cover of all time, Tim McGraw's version of "When the Stars Go Blue."

And she looked straight into Andrew's eyes as she sang the simple song with no extra flourishes or runs, as she vowed to follow him whenever he got lonely, whenever the stars went blue.

Before the last note was out of her mouth, he was reaching up and pulling her down from the stage and into his arms.

"You're amazing," he whispered, before drawing her even closer for a slow dance.

Perhaps sensing the changed mood in the honky tonk, the band played slow country songs until they finally exhausted and had to take a break. It seemed to Roxxy that Andrew would have kept on dancing, except Walt cut in, wanting to talk to her about whether she was interested in singing professionally, because he knew some people, and could introduce her to them.

"I'm really not interested," she answered, working hard

to keep the bemusement out of her voice.

He handed her his card. "Well, any time you want to come back, just let me know. I haven't heard a singer cover songs that good in a lifetime of Sundays."

Then it was time to go. Despite the late hour, Andrew made love to her slowly and passionately, like he wanted the night to last forever. She couldn't blame him, because she wanted the night to last forever, too. When they finally both came at the same time, it felt like the last perfect note for a song they'd created together.

The next day they kissed outside the house until Jeb arrived to drive Andrew to the airport. Their parting was sweet, with lots of "I'll miss you's" and "I love you's." Andrew assured her again and again he would call her every day, at least two times a day, for the week he was gone, and then he whispered in her ear that he would "fuck her so good" when he returned, that she should keep her pussy nice and warm, masturbate to thoughts of him every night, until he was back to do the job himself. He left her waving after him on the porch, her pants a sticky mess from his hot words.

Yes, Andrew Sinclair was like the biggest, best bowl of ice cream she'd ever had, and he kept on offering her things she wanted more than anything. Sex, college, a job, a life with him that might even include marriage at some point.

But she didn't have the ultimate spoon. She wasn't really Layla. And when he found this out, she knew she'd lose the best thing she'd ever had.

CHAPTER 20

ROXXY fully expected to be outted by whoever came to take her back to New York. And she was actually beginning to appreciate that the jig would be up while Andrew was out of town. That meant she'd never have to see the look on his face when he discovered how deeply she had misled him and that his dream reunion had happened with a woman who had been lying to him from day one.

"I was in a dishonest marriage for years, I'm not going to start out with you like that," he'd said. A nauseous mix of guilt and dread bubbled in Roxxy's stomach. How angry would he be when he discovered that was exactly how they'd started out?

Imagining Andrew's reaction to her duplicity soon became unbearable, and it made everything from working with the children's program to talking with him on the phone that much more painful. It got to the point where she couldn't wait for the D.A.'s people to come and get her already, just so this whole ordeal would be over.

Only they didn't come and get her. Every time a new car came down the dusty road leading up to the ranch, Roxxy expected it to be her ride home, but it was always a guest or a staff member or a delivery. After four days of walking around in a tight brace of tension and anticipation, Roxxy couldn't take it anymore.

This time the D.A. didn't chastise her when he answered the phone. As it turned out, "We're having a little bit of trouble finding your bodyguard."

"What?" she asked.

"We stopped by the address your mother gave us and found a whole bedroom dedicated to you, pictures and candles and everything. It was like walking into a movie cliché. Never seen anything like it. We got into his computer and found out he booked a flight to Canada, scheduled to return tomorrow, but somehow I doubt he'll be using the second part of that ticket. Anyway, we're working with Canadian authorities to track him down, but unlike in the movies, international searches are always red tape cluster fucks, so it's taking a while."

Roxxy's heart dropped into her stomach. How could she have so misjudged the man she'd trusted with her life for so many years? "So he's still out there, looking for me?"

"Yes, I'm afraid he is. The guy's computer system is state of the art. He has a half-finished degree in computer science, and he knows what you look like underneath the makeup. No doubt he could track you down easy if you appear anywhere on the grid. That's why it's more important than ever that you stay put and don't tell a soul who you are."

Roxxy swallowed past the knot in her throat. "I'm sorry, sir, but I can't do that. The man I'm staying with— honesty is very important to him. He's told me that since day one, and I can't keep lying to him."

"What are you talking about? You're a celebrity. The only people who lie more than you are politicians."

"Yes, but—"

"Are you trying to tell me you can keep your identity secret from millions of people, but keeping your mouth closed for the few days it takes to catch this guy is a 'can't do?'"

Roxxy twisted the cord of the phone around her finger. "I know it doesn't make any sense to you. But I have to tell him. He's a very honorable man and he deserves better than this."

"He'll probably be honored when he finds out he helped keep a celebrity from harm. And it's not like we're not going to compensate him for his time and your lodgings."

"I know," she said, "But some things can't be paid for with money. He taught me that."

The D.A. let out a deep sigh. "Oh, Christ, I should have seen this coming when you called saying we had to reassign you because he wasn't being nice enough to you. You think you're in love with him, don't you?"

"More than think it," Roxxy admitted. No, she thought forlornly to herself, being in love with Andrew Sinclair was something she knew down to her very soul.

"Okay, you've already proven yourself to be more idiotic than probably ninety-nine percent of the people we've had come through my office, so let me just break this down for you like you're a child," the D.A. said. "I know you said earlier that it felt like you had stepped into an episode of *Days of Our Lives*, but you are not currently in a soap opera. This guy lives in the middle of Nowhere, Montana. After the thrill of sex with somebody who doesn't know who you are goes away, trust me, you're going to get bored with him real fast."

"I won't," she said. "But you're right I have been living in a fantasy. And I know he's not going to want me when he finds out who I really am. But I have to tell him. Not because I think this is going to have a happy ending, but because it's the right thing to do. I know that sounds suspicious coming from somebody who measured right and wrong in ticket sales up until two weeks ago. But I've changed. He's changed me. And I have to tell him."

The D.A. cursed. "Fine, but if lover boy turns around and starts shooting his mouth off to everybody and his cousin about how he got off with Roxxy RoxX and leads

Dexter straight to your door, don't say I didn't warn you."

"No," she answered. "I'd never say you didn't give me plenty of warning about that, sir."

She hung up first this time, knowing it would be the last call she made to the D.A. She was done being bossed around. And no matter what happened with Andrew, she was done asking the D.A. for any more help.

It took several minutes and even more calming breaths before she was able to pick up the phone again and call Andrew.

"Hey, sweetheart," he said. He sounded sleepy. "At least I think it's my sweetheart calling from the house phone. Mrs. Garcia, is that you?"

"No," she said, laughing despite herself. "It's me. Mrs. Garcia isn't here yet. How are you?"

"You woke me up from a very nice dream."

"Oh, no. I'm sorry."

"It's okay, I needed to get up in a few minutes anyway. Plus, the dream was about you. Maybe you can help me finish it. What are you wearing?"

"Just a t-shirt and panties."

"No bra underneath?"

"No."

"Good, that's exactly what you were wearing in the dream. Except in the dream, you were curled up on your side, touching yourself because you missed me so bad. Is that true, sweetheart? Do you miss me?"

Roxxy squirmed. "I miss you a lot."

"Do you know what I'd do to you if I was there right now?"

"I imagine you'd kiss me on the back of the neck," she said. "Then you'd take my hand out of my pussy and replace it with your own."

"That's right. Your hand's been doing too much work

with me gone. Time to give it a rest."

"But maybe it doesn't want a rest. Maybe all my hand wants to do is wrap itself around your cock and show it how much I missed you."

He groaned a little, and she could hear the sounds of him shifting in bed.

Just the thought of Andrew on a bed in his hotel room jerking off to visions of her in Montana, had her rushing to get her own hand inside her panties.

"There's so much pre-cum coming out of your dick. I love how you feel in my hand. So hard. I think my mouth wants a taste, too."

He gave a sharp intake of breath. She could hear his hand moving in the background.

"Is it okay if I put my mouth down there?"

"Yes, wrap your lips around my dick and remember to open wide and relax your throat, so you get it all in. But first, do me a favor and turn around. Put your pussy over my face, so I can taste you, too."

Now her fingers started to move faster. Andrew's words were so potent, she could almost feel his tongue inside her, lapping at her pussy folds.

"Oh, sweetheart, this is why it's dangerous to keep your pussy shaved. I can see your clit's being naughty again, all big and swollen, demanding my attention. I'm going to have to suck on it to get it to go down."

Her hips bucked against her hand, just like they did whenever Andrew sucked on her clit.

She bit her lip. "Oh, you know how I get. If you don't stop, I'm going to come soon. And I'm having so much fun, working my mouth up and down on your dick. Please don't make me stop. It tastes so good."

"Oh, fuck, sweetheart." She could hear his bed creaking under the ministrations of his hand. "Come, come now, or I'm going to come first."

Against her wishes, she burst apart, creaming onto her own fingers. And her soft cry must have set him off, too, because he let out a long guttural groan.

A few seconds later he said, "Good morning, sweetheart."

She giggled, basking in her own afterglow. "Good morning, Andrew."

"Well, it looks like I really need to get in the shower now. I'm a mess. Thanks for calling."

"No problem," she said. But then reality came crashing back in. "But I actually called for a reason."

"Are you okay?" he asked, his voice suddenly serious. "Is there something wrong at the ranch?"

"I'm fine. The ranch is fine, too. But…" She cleared her throat. "I have something I wanted to talk with you about."

"Sweetheart, I feel like an ass rushing you off the phone after what we just did, but now I've only got fifteen minutes to get ready for my next meeting."

"Oh, okay," Roxxy, said, scrambling to keep up. "Maybe I could call you later tonight then?"

"Actually I managed to move all of tomorrow's meetings to today, so it's back to back, then I'm having dinner and drinks with the C.E.O of a foundation I'm hoping will give us some grant money. And then I've got to get some sleep, because I'm headed to the airport early in the morning to catch the first flight out of D.C."

She blinked. "You're flying out tomorrow morning? But you aren't due back for two more days."

She could hear his smile on the other side of the phone. "I wasn't kidding about missing you, sweetheart. I'll be back at the ranch before breakfast. So we can talk then, okay?"

"Okay," she said, her voice small.

"Love you, sweetheart. I'm going to show you how much tomorrow, all day, so don't make any plans."

She laughed, but it sounded weak, even to her ears. "I love you, too."

She hung up the phone with a sigh. Apparently, she wouldn't be able to get away with leaving it to others to tell Andrew what she had done after she'd left, or even telling him over the phone.

No apparently, Fate seemed hell bent on making sure when she ruined the best thing that had ever happened to her, she'd be doing it in person.

CHAPTER 21

ANDREW was still feeling guilty when Jeb picked him up from the airport the next morning. Layla had asked him to talk yesterday, and he'd practically shoved her off of the line, and right after phone sex at that. Yes, he'd done it, because he was rushing into meetings in order to get back home to her sooner. But he didn't want her to think sex was all he cared about when it came to their relationship.

The sex was, he had to admit, outstanding. Better than anything he'd ever imagined when they'd dated the first time around and she'd asked him to wait. But their current relationship was definitely about more than that. When they were in college, he'd liked Layla because she was sweet and smart, and really cute. It had also helped that he was going through a small rebellious phase. So he'd not only recently dumped his blond society girlfriend, he'd managed to land someone who was the complete opposite of her, someone who he really liked, and someone his parents did not approve of. It felt like a total win.

Dating Layla in college had been a little like dating Mother Teresa. She wasn't like any of the other girls he had gone out with. There wasn't a cynical bone in her body, she volunteered on a regular basis, and had a kind word for everybody.

When the old Layla looked at him, she didn't see a pampered rich kid who, unlike her, had been given everything in life. She saw the best in him, and it made him want to be a better person. He respected the hell out of her, so he watched himself carefully to make sure he never said anything untoward to or around her. He didn't pressure her or demand anything more than she was willing to give. More than anything, he wanted to be the man she saw when she looked up at him, which had been part of the reason he let her go when she asked for his blessing to marry Nathan.

But then she'd reappeared out of the blue on his ranch, way sexier and much funnier than he remembered. She'd completely wreaked havoc on his self-control. He'd been acting the gentleman all his life, but with this new Layla he felt stripped bare, like he had no choice but to be the real version of himself around her. She seemed to relish getting under his skin, and responded to his dirty talk like she had an engine inside her primed only for him.

He wanted her. Not just her body, but all of her. He also wanted to spend the rest of his life with her. He patted the ring inside his suit pocket. He knew it might seem like it was too soon to others and to Layla herself even. But in his opinion, it wasn't soon enough. He'd known he'd wanted to be with her permanently ever since their first night together in the barn.

He wanted to have kids with her, and make Sinclair Township happen with her. For the rest of his life he wanted her by his side. He just hoped she felt the same way and that her divorce from Nathan hadn't left her feeling bitter about marriage like it did with some women.

He was shaken from his thoughts by his phone going off just as they were pulling up to the front gate of the ranch. It was Nathan. He sent the call to voicemail again, knowing he'd eventually have to call his brother back and let him know Layla was with him now. But he knew his brother. If Nathan still wanted Layla even a little bit, he'd come out to Montana and fight Andrew tooth and nail for her. That was the kind of predator he was. But Andrew wouldn't let him win this time. He loved Layla too much, and he'd be damned if he concede her to Nathan again.

As if summoned by his heated thoughts of her, there

was Layla at the front gate, waving to him. He waved back and got out of the truck. He frowned when he noticed her hair was once again large, with kinky curls that fell all the way to her shoulders—the way she'd worn it when she was with Nathan.

Admittedly, he didn't know much about black women's hair, but he knew that there wasn't any place nearby where she could have gotten a weave. And she'd never struck him as the kind of person to wear wigs. Also, was it him, or had she gained a little weight since the last time he'd seen her? Not that he minded—he'd take Layla at any size. She just looked…different.

But then she was running up to him and wrapping her arms around him in a big hug. "Oh, Andrew! I was so worried. It's good to see you again."

He laughed. "No need to worry. The flight got in just fine. But I missed you, too. Come here."

He cupped his hand around the back of her neck and kissed her with all the passion he'd been storing up the five days they'd been apart.

But then he felt her pushing against his chest. "What? Andrew, stop! Let me go!"

Shit, he must have accidentally triggered her again. He stopped kissing her, but held her firm. "Breathe, sweetheart. It's me Andrew. It's okay—"

She slapped him, so hard his head cracked sideways.

"I can't believe you!!" she all but screeched. And the next thing he knew, she was walking away in a huff, back toward the house.

What the hell?

ROXXY DID NOT SLEEP WELL the night before Andrew was due home. First, there was the dream about

Andrew flipping out and calling her every name under the sun before kicking her off his ranch.

Then there was the dream about Andrew, the entire ranch staff, and all of its guests gathering around her in a circle and chanting, "Liar! Liar! Liar!"

Then came the worst dream of all, the one that shook her up more than the other two combined. In that one she explained everything to Andrew, only to have him wrap her up in his arms and say, "I just want to be with you. I don't care who you are." That dream had nearly broken her heart when she'd woken up only to discover it wasn't real.

She took a shower, but still felt dirty as she donned the t-shirt and jeans Andrew had bought for her. The thought of her usual morning tea turned her stomach. No, this was a coffee kind of morning, and she just hoped she could get at least one cup in before she had to make her confession to Andrew.

Luck, however, was not on her side. She found Andrew, standing in the middle of the living room with his phone to his ear. "Hey, since you weren't answering any of my calls, I decided to pay you a visit. I'm at the ranch, so call me back."

She paused on the bottom step, wondering who he was talking to. There was something different about him this morning. His voice seemed more cynical than she remembered, and the sandy highlights had disappeared from his hair, leaving it darker. This gave him a hawkish air, and somehow he didn't seem like the man who had left here just a few days ago.

Roxxy tried to shake off the uneasy feeling. It was just nerves, she assured herself. But still, she stood there awkwardly, not quite sure how to alert him to her presence in the room.

A kiss, she thought to herself. One last kiss, before she had to destroy everything between them.

So she covered his eyes from behind.

"Layla," he said, "I know it's you. Who else would be covering my eyes?"

"No, senor," she said. "It is I, Mrs. Garcia."

"That is a terrible accent," he informed her.

Then he surprised her by capturing her hands by the wrists and turning around, so her hands were trapped tight behind his neck. Suddenly the kiss she had thought she was initiating was completely taken over by him.

Roxxy squeaked a little bit. This kiss wasn't like any of the ones he'd given her before. Usually Andrew's kisses were steady and insistent, like he was patiently pulling every ounce of passion she had to give out of her. But this one was nothing short of a hostile takeover, and for many confusing moments, it felt to Roxxy like she was being kissed by a complete stranger.

IT TOOK ANDREW A FEW running steps to catch up with Layla. "What the hell, Layla?"

"I should be asking you the same thing," she shot back, her face tight with anger. "What did you think you were doing back there?"

"Kissing the girl I love. I thought you loved me too, otherwise why are you here?"

"To see you. I was worried about you. That's why I'm here, not to have you shove your tongue down my throat. I thought we had come to an understanding about this."

"I thought we had, too," Andrew said, his mind roaring with rage. "I don't understand why you would slap me when I tried to kiss you."

She shook her head at him. "I love Nathan, okay. I

don't want to hurt you. But I've already told you I loved Nathan. You were at our wedding. You were his best man. I can't believe you would do this."

It was like his worst nightmare came true. Layla was looking at him like he was some sort of psycho, like she couldn't believe he'd think she'd ever pick him over his brother. "You came to me!" Andrew yelled at her. "You're the one who got my hopes up." A thought occurred to him and it stopped him in his tracks. "Wait a minute, did you hit your head again? Did you forget you said you loved me?"

Now the look in her eyes morphed from anger to pity. "When I said I loved you, I thought it was understood I loved you as my brother-in-law, not like I love Nathan."

They came to the house then and she jogged up the stairs. Andrew couldn't figure out if she was trying to take refuge in the house or put space between them. Maybe both.

But then once she was at the door, she turned back to him and said, "Listen, I'm sorry I came. It's obviously caused you some hurt and confusion. But I was worried about you." She put her hand on the doorknob. "Come inside and we'll all talk."

"No," he said, his face a storm cloud of emotion. "I dumped my girlfriend to be with you, Layla. Do you really think this is something we can just talk out?"

Layla looked both confused and distressed now. "Nathan's inside. Let's all just sit down and talk about this."

His face screwed up. "So that's what this is all about? Nathan's back and now you're ready to toss me aside. Does he know what we did, how many times we fucked all over this ranch? What you told me at the ski lodge? You don't do that with someone you love like a brother-in-law—at least not outside a porno."

Her eyes widened in horror. "Okay, Andrew. If you care about me at all, please come inside. Nathan will call somebody for you, because I think you need professional help."

He stalked up the stairs toward her. "Professional help my ass. I'm not going to let you play the victim this time, Layla. I'm going in there, and I'm going to tell Nathan what happened between us. I love you, and maybe Nathan's managed to brainwash you, but I know you love me. I'm not backing down this time."

He shoved open the door, but then stopped short when he saw his brother in the living room in a heavy make out session with a woman who looked exactly like the one standing beside him, only with shorter hair.

She must have seen them out of the corner of her eye, because she pulled away from Nathan, her face awash in horror.

"Good idea, we don't want to start anything we can't finish before my brother gets home." He then blinked at her. "Did you go and get a hair cut somewhere? And when did you change clothes?"

Then, he, too, seemed to finally sense Andrew's and Layla's presence at the door.

He looked between longhaired Layla and shorthaired Layla before saying, "Holy shit. All this time, we thought you were out here running a ranch, and you were cloning my wife."

Andrew's heart became a stone in his chest. "There's no such thing as a human clone you can replicate as an adult from scratch," he said to his brother. His eyes then landed on shorthaired Layla. "Who are you?"

Shorthaired Layla winced. "You know, I never, ever name drop. But would this situation be helped at all if I told you I was the chart-topping super star, and international singing sensation, Roxxy RoxX?"

CHAPTER 22

ROXXY'S announcement was greeted with stunned silence, which she guessed meant no one believed her.

And that was confirmed when Andrew repeated, this time louder and even angrier, *"Who are you?"*

"Not Layla, obviously," she said. Then the whole story came out in a quick rush of words. "And I'm really sorry I lied to you. But here's the deal. I was being stalked by somebody who turned out to be my former bodyguard, and I needed a place to stay. So Steve Kass flew me out here to Montana to hide out at your ranch. However, I sort of accidentally got drunk, then I woke up here, and you thought I was Layla. And I would have told you the truth, but the *district attorney of New York—* by the way, he's not a very nice guy *at all*, and I will not be voting for him in the next election—anyway, he told me I had to stay put and to maintain the cover story you'd given me. You see people couldn't know who I really was, because if word got out, it would lead the stalker straight to me. So I had to lie to you and everybody else here. Again, I'm really sorry."

Another moment of stunned silence, then Nathan said, "Oh, I get it, the cloning program didn't quite work and now you've got a clone with mental problems."

"But you look just like me." The real Layla chose this moment to step forward.

"Yeah, I do." Roxxy looked the other woman up and down, her own matching eyes wide with amazement. "When I first came here, I thought Andrew was just one of those white people who couldn't tell black people apart. But now that I'm looking at you for real..."

Layla stepped closer to her and tentatively reached out.

"Your eyes, your face. You look *exactly* like me."

"I know," Roxxy said to her. "It's kind of freaking me out, too."

"But how is this possible?" Layla asked. "You even have my same voice. Except I can't sing. And you say you can? To the point you've made a good living off of it?"

"C'mon, Layla," Nathan said. "You can't believe anything she says. For all you know, she saw a picture of you in the paper when everything between you and Andrew's wife went down, got plastic surgery to look just like you, and came out here to seduce Andrew. She's most likely living in some kind of sick fantasy world."

Roxxy glared at the man who was obviously Andrew's identical twin brother, finding it hard to believe anyone in her right mind would choose this guy over Andrew. "I'm not lying and I don't have mental problems. I really am Roxxy RoxX."

"Prove it then. Show us some ID."

Roxxy rolled her eyes. "I gave my wallet to Steve Kass. It's probably still in the safe in his New York office. But my real name is Roxxanne Weathers."

Layla's eyes widened. "Weathers. That was my mother's maiden name."

"She could have looked that up, too. Easily," Nathan said. He came over and put his arm around his wife's shoulders, as if to protect her from Roxxy's obvious insanity.

"I'm not making it up. I had no idea who you were before I met Andrew. And believe me, it was taking everything in me not to ask after your full back story, because it sounds like a doozy."

Layla opened her mouth, but Nathan said, "She's lying. Just like Andrew's dead wife lied to get you to follow her into that library. She's playing on your kind nature." He glared at Roxxy. "But I won't allow you to take advantage of my wife. She's already been through too much. I don't know who you are or what kind sick, perverted fantasy brought you here, but—"

Roxxy cut him off in favor of talking to Layla. "Wait a minute, you said your mother's maiden name was Weathers? That can't be a coincidence. Was her first name Shirelle?"

"No, it was Linda. But her middle initial was 'S.'" Layla answered. "My father, who passed away a few years ago, told me she died in a car accident when I was three."

Roxxy frowned. "That's weird, because my mom told me my father died overseas when I was three. That's also when we moved out to New York. Do you have any pictures of your mom?"

"No," Layla said, shaking her head. "My father died a few years ago, but I didn't find any pictures of her. Not even a wedding picture."

"Sounds like a burn job to me. My mom didn't have any pictures of my dad either, and I always thought that was weird, since they were married." Roxxy said. "Maybe they both lied to us. Maybe your dad got rid of all the pictures of her because he was mad at her for leaving or something. Maybe that's why he told you she was dead."

Layla came out from under Nathan's arm and took a hold of her hand. "Are you saying my mom, our mom, is out there and still alive?"

"Layla, do not let her play this game with you. She's already admitted to being a fake and a liar. Now she's telling you exactly what you want to hear."

Andrew folded his arms. "Just like she pretended to be the woman I wanted her to be."

Roxxy turned to Andrew and said, "I did lie. And I'm sorry Andrew, more sorry than I can ever express. But I'm not lying now. Not about this. And I can prove it."

She ran over to the phone in the living room and punched in the only number she had ever bothered to memorize.

"Hello?" came Shirelle's voice over the line. She sounded suspicious, probably because the call was coming from a weird area code. She doubted her mother got many calls from Montana.

"Shirelle, it's me," Roxxy said.

"Oh, thank goodness. Thank the Lord. I've been so worried about you, especially when they came around here asking about Dexter. You know they think he's the one who murdered Mabel and that poor assistant D.A. who was supposed to be escorting you to safety. I tried to get them to tell me where you were but they wouldn't, even though I'm your mother."

Roxxy waited for her to take a breath before saying, "I'm standing here with a woman named Layla Matthews, a woman who looks so much like me, it's obvious we're twins. And her husband is accusing me of being some psycho, who purposefully got plastic surgery to look like her…"

"Oh no," her mother said. "I never meant for you to find out this way. Just tell me where you are and I'll come out and explain everything."

"I can't believe this, Shirelle! Did you seriously neglect to tell me I had a twin sister?"

"Please, I promise you, I can explain everything. I will get on the next plane out there, just tell me where you are."

"I'm at the Sinclair Ranch in Montana," Roxxy said between gritted teeth. "Look it up and get out here with your explanation, fast."

Roxxy all but threw the receiver back in its cradle. "She said she's coming and she'll explain everything," she said to Layla. "I'm sorry, she's always been a liar, but so is everyone else in the music business. I never imagined she was hiding something this big from me."

"Now I think really do believe you," Layla said, tears coming to her eyes. "My dad wasn't that great with the truth himself."

Roxxy looked at Layla and for a moment, the situation with Andrew temporarily fell away as her heart swelled with love for a woman she'd only met five minutes ago. She, Roxxane Weathers, who had always felt alone in the world, despite her mother and the team of people surrounding her at all times, had a sister. A twin sister. "I have a sister," she whispered.

Tears spilled over in Layla's eyes. "I've always wanted a sister. And, you're famous. That's so cool, I can't believe it."

Roxxy shrugged, chagrinned. "Being famous isn't all that great. I mean I am currently hiding out from a stalker. And even before that, I was planning to get out of the business all together. I was supposed to start at University of Southern California this fall. I want to get a progressive degree in public administration, so I can do non-profit work after I get out."

"USC, wow! You must be so smart."

Roxxy blushed under Layla's effusive praise. "It's a little easier to get in if you're famous."

"Still…that's really brave to change career paths at our age. I'm proud of you."

"You're pretty cool yourself. I mean you're a physical therapist, right? And other than the asshole husband, you seem like a really great person. From what I've heard, everybody loves you."

"Oh, whoever told you that is really kind…"

She trailed off then, perhaps realizing, as Roxxy had in

that moment, that the person who had told her that was still in the room, and moreover had been under the impression she was Layla for the past two weeks.

Roxxy turned back to Andrew. "Again, I just want to say how sorry I am. I know you're thinking right now that you were sleeping with an imposter, but please believe me when I tell you—I've been pretending to be somebody else, somebody cooler and sexier than I really am nearly all of my adult life. But the person who's been with you, the woman who fell in love with you in under two weeks. She's real. And I have never felt more real than when I was with you."

But the way Andrew was looking at her, it was like a stranger was staring her down. "You lied to me," he said. "You lied to me every single day you spent under my roof."

"Yeah, I did," she admitted. "But I didn't lie to you about the important things. Like how I felt about you. I never lied about that."

In what Roxxy could guess was an unfamiliar gesture of solidarity, Nathan placed a hand on Andrew's shoulder.

"I can see how you'd be taken in by her. She looks just like Layla and maybe she really believes what she's saying. We'll give her mother a few hours to get here, then we'll take it from there."

Andrew looked at Roxxy like she was a piece of toxic waste, then he gave a stiff nod, acquiescing to Nathan's suggestion.

Roxxy reached out to Andrew, who had said goodbye to her with such love in his eyes the last time they saw each other. That now felt like eons ago.

"Don't touch me," he said, his voice hard as nails. "You can stay here until your mother arrives, then you're leaving with her. I don't care who you fucking are. I never want to see you again."

CHAPTER 23

"I don't care who you fucking are. I never want to see you again."

Andrew's words reverberated through her head over the next few hours, which Roxxy spent alone, after once again taking solace in the hay barn. But this time when the barn door opened it wasn't Andrew, but Layla.

"Oh good, you're here," she said. "A few of the ranch hands told me you might be."

Roxxy winced, thinking of the ever-present ranch hands, all of whom had thought she was the woman now asking how to find her. "Is everyone mad at me?"

"No," Layla answered, sitting down beside her. "Just really, really curious. You can kind of tell it's taking every ounce of politeness they have not to grill me about what's going on. But it's not so bad. You should come back out. We could go to dinner. You probably haven't had anything to eat all day, right?"

Roxxy smiled despite herself. "You're being really nice. And I have no idea why after what I did. You should be even madder at me than Andrew."

Layla rubbed her back. "Andrew's not just mad, he's embarrassed. And he feels like you tricked him on purpose."

"I didn't," Roxxy said.

"I know you didn't. I believe you."

Roxxy blinked. "You believe me?"

"Yes, and I think Andrew will eventually come around, too. We just have to give him some time. Having your mom come and tell us the whole story will definitely help." Layla cut herself off. "I guess I should be calling her our mom. I already feel connected to you, but I'm finding it hard to believe my mom is still out there living and breathing."

Now Roxxy reached to take Layla's hand. "She is, but don't get your hopes up when it comes to her. She's not exactly what you'd call maternal, and growing up with her was no picnic. She makes other stage moms look like Suzy Homemaker."

"But she raised you, right?" Layla said, hope burning in her eyes. "And you're successful?"

"Yeah, she raised me but it's looking like she abandoned you. And if I know my mom, she'll say it's because you weren't able to sing at the age of three. My earliest memories are of going out on audition after audition. And I have a feeling she's going to dump me like a useless boyfriend once she finds out I'm going back to school." Roxxy didn't realize how bitter she was about all of this until she said the words, "If I wasn't making her a ton of money, I don't think she'd want anything to do with me."

Layla gave her a sympathetic look. "Let's just wait and see, okay? Sometimes people come off a certain way, but then they surprise you. For example, even Nathan's brother thought he was a jerk who only cared about himself. To tell you the truth, even I kind of got that vibe off of Nathan when we first met. But then he turned out to be the most loving man. I feel so lucky we found each other again and got married. I've never been so happy."

Roxxy didn't answer, just gave Layla a sideways look. Nathan had accused Roxxy of being delusional when she finally told everyone the truth, but he might want to look at his own wife. That man *was* a jerk, and Layla acted like he'd hung the stars in the sky. Still, she'd rather have a crazy-but-really-nice sister than none at all, so she went back to Andrew.

"You really think Andrew will forgive me someday? He made it pretty clear he has no time in his life for liars."

Layla snorted. "Andrew's a very kind man, but he's no saint. About a year into our college relationship, I started developing feelings for Nathan that I could no longer deny. But when I tried to break it off with Andrew, he kissed me in an attempt to show me he was just as passionate as Nathan. Nathan walked in on us and jumped to the conclusion that I had slept with him but decided to stay with Andrew, and he ran out before I could explain. Shortly after, I got pushed down the stairs and lost my memory of both Andrew and Nathan and everything that had gone down between us. Nathan continued to believe I had chosen Andrew over him for ten years, and Andrew never told him the truth. He even got married to his wife, Diana, and let Nathan suffer the entire time because he didn't think Nathan deserved me."

As much as she loved her sister, Roxxy had to point out, "I'm kind of with Andrew here. You're great. Your husband definitely doesn't deserve you."

Layla shook her head with stubborn pride. "I know he's a little rough around the edges and harsh. But I love him, and Andrew knew that. He purposefully kept us apart for nearly a decade. Then it all came to a head when he asked his wife for a divorce. She thought we were back together and tried to shoot me. If I hadn't rushed her at the last minute, and she didn't accidentally end up shooting herself, I'd be dead right now instead of sitting here talking to you."

"Whoa," Roxxy said. She had known the back story everyone kept referring to would be dramatic, but—"Are you sure you're not living in a soap opera come to life? Because that's some cray-cray drama right there."

Layla laughed. "I know, right. And now I've got a

famous twin? I'm surprised Lifetime hasn't made a movie about me yet."

Roxxy laughed, too. "I know people. We could make it happen."

Layla giggled even harder. "No, that's okay. People are still stopping me on the street to ask me about that story with Andrew's wife. I really not trying to invite any more attention."

When their laughter finally died down, Layla said, "My main point is, if I can forgive Andrew for all of that, then he can forgive you for not telling him the whole truth from the beginning. Andrew has been very careful with women since his last wife turned out to have…" Layla, whom Roxxy was beginning to see, was unfailingly kind, searched for the most polite term, "…major issues. And don't forget, he dumped his girlfriend to be with you."

Another wave of guilt. "I didn't ask him to do that."

"Exactly. There has to be more to his feelings than thinking I was available. The way he talked to me when he thought I was you—there was more passion in his anger than I'd seen from him in our entire relationship. And I saw the look on his face when he walked in on you and Nathan kissing. You really hurt him."

"And that's a good thing?" Roxxy asked, shaking her head in confusion.

"Yes!" Layla insisted. "When you love somebody, I mean really love them, then you don't shrug your shoulders and wish them well when they tell you they want to be with someone else. Andrew loved me, but when I asked him that second time to let me go in order to be with Nathan, he didn't put up a fight. Like at all. And even when I admitted to cheating on him with Nathan, he was more concerned with winning me back from his brother than what I'd done. He never really got angry with me. It was more like he was angry because Nathan had one-upped him."

Layla patted Roxxy on the back. "Just let your mom—our mom explain and Andrew will eventually come around." She put her arm around Roxxy's shoulders and squeezed. "I have a good feeling about you two."

For the first time that day, Roxxy started to feel a little optimistic herself. "Really?"

"Yes, really." Layla gave her a bright smile. "Just wait and see."

And Roxxy found herself smiling back. She didn't know if Layla's prediction would come true, but she could already tell one thing for sure. She was going to really love having a sister.

WHEN A KNOCK SOUNDED ON HIS OFFICE DOOR a few hours after the look-a-like farce went down, Andrew half-expected it to be Layla—the real Layla, not the one who had been duping him for weeks now. The real Layla was the kind of person who couldn't bear to see others in pain and might insist on coming upstairs to comfort him. She wouldn't realize that just looking at her was painful for him now, because it reminded him of the fantasy he'd been peddled and how stupid he'd been.

He didn't want to hurt Layla's feelings but called out, "Leave me alone until further notice."

His brother came strolling into the room a few seconds later, like Andrew hadn't requested that the person at the door go away. Typical Nathan.

"So you like to sulk in your office, too," Nathan said, looking around. "When I was getting back together with Layla, I clocked a lot of hours in mine. Sometimes it felt like the only place that made any goddamn sense."

Andrew slumped in his chair. "If you've come to gloat, save it. You can't make me feel any worse than I already do."

Nathan dropped into a guest chair. "Please don't use the word 'can't' with me. You know how hard I find it to back down from a challenge."

Andrew ignored the bait his brother was trying to dangle in front of him. With him and Nathan, it was a thin line between words and a physical fight. But Andrew was feeling too beat down himself to fight with his brother in either way right now, so he stayed silent, waiting for Nathan to get to the point of his visit.

Nathan shrugged. "Look, I promised Layla before our wedding that I'd work on my relationship with you and I haven't been doing all that good a job at it. Believe me, she was livid when I told her I'd been trying to get a hold of you for two weeks after you called me, and you hadn't returned any of my calls. She's the one who insisted we fly out here and make sure you were all right. Good thing she did, too, or that girl would have gone on tricking you indefinitely."

"So you're here to get a thank you for coming out here unannounced?" Andrew asked him.

"No, I'm here because you're still my brother, and even if you did get it on with a crazy clone of my wife, I don't like when other people take advantage of you. I'm thinking we should sue her for fraud. Take her for everything she has, so she thinks twice before ever pulling this stunt again."

Andrew was strangely touched by his brother's words. "Thanks, but I don't want revenge. I just want her to go away, so I can forget any of this ever happened."

"Okay, how about if I work the revenge angle, and then let you know when it's done? You'd be surprise how much better revenge can make you feel."

"You mean like when you got Layla to agree to leave Pittsburgh forever, because you were so angry at her when you thought she'd chosen me over you? How did that little piece of revenge work out? Last I checked she was still living in Pittsburgh, and with you no less."

Nathan glared at him. "Not the same thing at all. Layla was a victim. This chick came out here with every attention of playing you."

Andrew shook his head. He wished he could get himself as worked up as his brother right now. He'd love to concentrate on revenge and nothing else. But he couldn't get past what had happened in the living room.

When he'd walked in on Fake Layla kissing Nathan, he'd want to punch his brother for even daring to touch her. And even after he realized this woman wasn't really Layla, it hadn't stopped him from wanting to throw her over his shoulder, take her up to his room, and show her in every way it was him she wanted and not his brother.

And when she'd told that impossible story…

"I want it to be true," he confessed, though he'd made it a point throughout his life never, ever to share his feelings with his callous brother. "I want her to really be the witness Steve Kass was supposed to drop off with me, because if she really is who she says she is, then maybe I can forgive her." He shook his head. "You think this is all about me wanting to get with your wife, but believe me, I had let Layla go. I'd moved on. But then this woman showed up, and it was like nothing I've ever felt before. My dick gets hard every time she walks into the room. And she told me some things about herself, stuff I don't think anybody could make up. Plus, she can sing. I mean, really well. She got up on stage at this bar we were at and she had the whole crowd in the palm of her hand."

Nathan rolled his eyes. "Congratulations, the woman you were sleeping with is not only a liar and a psycho, but also an *American Idol* reject."

Andrew didn't watch much television, but even he got what Nathan was trying to say. Being able to sing well didn't make Fake Layla the music superstar she was claiming to be.

"I think I knew deep down she wasn't really Layla, because Layla and I got along, but we never had anything close to the chemistry I had with this woman."

Nathan shrugged. "I get it. She's hot. Believe me, I had a hard time keeping my hands off Layla myself. But you've got to understand, her story has about a one and a million chance of being true. If it is, that means, somehow of all the places, this rock star who no one has seen without her makeup could have been sent, it's to the brother-in-law of the twin sister she didn't know she had. The odds of that happening are—"

"Astronomical," Andrew finished for him, a dark cloud once again settling over him. "I know."

But Nathan kept on going. "On the other hand, people become obsessed with people all the time—especially rich and famous people. We were all over the news when that stuff with Diana went down. Anyone could have glommed on to that story and started spinning a fantasy that got out of control. In any case, it's way more likely she's completely nuts than Layla's long lost twin sister."

He was right. Andrew knew Nathan was right. And it made him feel like a psycho himself to hold on to the hope that somehow fate had conspired to bring him the perfect woman in the form of Layla's long-lost twin. But he couldn't stop himself.

And when he saw a BMW pull up outside the front of the house, he sat up in his seat. A well put-together black woman climbed out of the car and looked around. Andrew stood up to get a better look at her. Even in the dim light of the setting sun, he could see she resembled Roxxy and Layla enough to have some family connection.

"She doesn't look old enough to be their mother," Nathan said, getting up to stand with him at the window.

Andrew's face became grim. "Let's go get some answers," he said to his brother.

CHAPTER 24

WHEN the door to the barn opened a second time, Roxxy stood up, because she thought it might be Andrew. But it was actually Nathan who came through the door followed by Shirelle and then, finally Andrew.

"Roxxanne!" her mother cried out when she saw her. She ran to Roxxy and engulfed her in a fierce hug. "Thank God, you're okay."

Roxxy was a little taken aback by her mother's enthusiastic greeting. Shirelle hadn't hugged her in years, especially not this tight. Maybe Layla had been right about people surprising you. "I'm fine. And thank you for coming," she said. "Now that you're here you can explain why you did what you did."

Her mother pulled back from her, shaking her head. "What are you talking about, Roxxane?"

"I'm talking about the twin sister you never told me about."

Shirelle squinted at Layla as if seeing her for the first time. "Oh my God, you're Layla Sinclair, aren't you?"

"Yes, I am," Layla said, obviously confused. "And I was under the impression you might be my mother. Our mother."

"Oh no," Shirelle said, backing away from Roxxy. "Roxxanne's been obsessed with you for awhile now, ever since she saw your story in the paper. And when she spent her life savings to get plastic surgery to look like you..."

"What?" Roxxy asked. "You're the one who's in love with plastic surgery. I don't even get botox!"

Shirelle went on like she hadn't even spoken. "I'm afraid, she became too much for our family to handle. We had her committed to a facility."

"Why are you lying?" Roxxy demanded, realizing now that her mother was seriously making up a story about her as opposed to telling everyone the truth.

Shirelle hung her head in what looked like abject sorrow. "Whenever I came to visit her at the facility, she'd be talking about you and how you should have picked Andrew Sinclair, because obviously he loved you."

"What?" Roxxy said. "No, I haven't! I never even heard of any of you before I came to the ranch."

Shirelle shook her head at Roxxy. "I still can't believe you did this to yourself, Roxxane. Now you look more like her than me and we're actually sisters."

"We are *not* sisters," Roxxy said, rolling her eyes. This wasn't the first time Shirelle had claimed to be her sister in front of an audience. "She's my mother, my extremely vain mother, and she's lying. I have no idea why."

Shirelle shook her head in apology to Layla. "I don't know what Roxxanne told you. And I hope it wasn't something too hurtful. But she's been off her meds for several weeks now, ever since she escaped from the group home. Did she also try to tell you she was Roxxy RoxX? That's who she was obsessed with before you, ever since she found out they both spelled their first name with two X's. In fact, part of the reason we were able to get her committed after her plastic surgery, was because she also violated the restraining order Roxxy had against her."

"What?!" Roxxy screamed the question this time. "I can't believe you. You'd do anything to keep me in the life you chose for me. Even lie about me being crazy?"

A thought suddenly occurred to Roxxy. "Oh my God, you're not just an off-the-chain stage mother. You're actually a sociopath. You probably knew what that label head was going to do to me when you sent me up there to meet with him. You knew and you sent me anyway, even though I was only sixteen."

Shirelle shook her head. "Oh, Roxxy, we've talked about this. That's why you have to stay on your meds. The paranoia, the hallucinations, they're not good for you, and look how much trouble you've caused these good people."

"'These good people?'" Roxxy mocked. "Maybe you're the one who should be taking acting lessons, because you sound like a bad Lifetime movie right now."

Shirelle thrust out a hand with a pill in it. "Please just take this. It will calm you down and then I can take you home."

"So now you're trying to dope me up again? Do you ever stop?" Roxxy could barely keep herself from clawing her mother's eyes out at that point. "I'm not taking any pills, and I'm most certainly not going anywhere with you."

"Please, Roxxy," her mother said with what sounded like real tears in her eyes. "You're my sister, and I've been worried sick about you for weeks now. Not sleeping, barely eating. I'm so tired. Just please take the pill, so we can go home."

"Stop with the crocodile tears, you controlling harpie," Roxxy said, feeling the urge to cry herself, but with frustration. "I'm sick to death of you trying to manipulate me. You are a terrible mother. You've always been a terrible mother, and if you think I'll ever pay you another dime of my money, you're—"

"Roxxanne!" the sound of Andrew saying her real name for the first time in their relationship, cut her short.

She looked up to find Andrew still standing near the door, his hands in fists at his side.

"Your sister's right," he said.

"She's not my sister," Roxxy started. "Layla is."

"I don't care who you think this woman is. Or who you

think you are. You've done enough damage here. You've hurt enough people, and I want you gone. If you have any decency at all, if you have even one not-crazy bone in your body, you will go with your sister and never come back here."

Roxxy turned to Layla for support, only to find her twin silently weeping into Nathan's chest.

She didn't believe her, Roxxy realized. No one believed her. She had basically given her mother the exact story she needed to get out of explaining why she abandoned Layla in the first place.

She gritted her teeth. "Fine," she said. "I'll go. But Andrew, Layla, and Nathan, I have one last thing to say before I do. I *am* a good person, a better person than I ever thought I could be. I found that out here. And I'm going to do amazing things. I'll start my own camp for underprivileged kids if necessary. But I will spend the rest of my life proving I'm not who you think I am right now."

She strode to the door. "And one last thing, nobody calls me 'Roxxanne' except my back-stabbing mother. My name is 'Roxxy.'"

And with one last look at the man she loved, the man she had thought loved her, Roxxy walked out with her head held high.

CHAPTER 25

LESS than thirty minutes after the scene in the barn with Layla/Roxxanne, the real Layla declared. "I'm going after her."

They were back in the living room where it had all started, and Layla got to her feet. "C'mon, Nathan. Your name's on the rental car, so you're going to have to drive me."

Nathan, who was nursing a tumbler of scotch, didn't move from the chair he was lounging in. "Sit down, Layla. The only place we're going in the next few hours is to get the couples' massage I booked for us at the spa. The one we both deserve after the day we've had."

Layla wrung her hands. "I've had a terrible feeling ever since she left. And now, I really think she was telling us the truth, Nathan. The look on her face as she was leaving, like she was so hurt none of us believed her."

"None of us believed her because she was obviously lying. Just like Nathan said she was. Her *real* sister confirmed that." Andrew pointed out.

"Well then, maybe there's something more we can do to help her. How good is the facility she's staying at if they let her escape? And I swear Roxxy was right about that lady's acting skills. Something about her didn't seem quite right. Don't you think she looked at me just a little too long, before she denied being my mother?"

Nathan sighed. "Layla, you know I love you more than anyone or anything else on the face of this Earth. But after what happened with Andrew's wife, I think we've established you're not a reliable judge of character."

"The fact that you married Nathan alone pretty much tells us that," Andrew said.

Nathan pointed at him. "I'm going to let you get away with that because you're hurting right now, and my time with Layla has turned me into a better person." He turned back to Layla. "But he's right. You're not exactly dealing aces when it comes to choosing who you associate with."

Layla made a little growly sound. "Ooh, I am so sick of you two patronizing me just because I almost got shot by Andrew's poor, mentally unstable wife. And I'm even more sick of people insulting my husband to my face. You are an amazing husband, a wonderful man, and quite frankly, the best lover I've had. Plus, you're gorgeous and really rich. I hit the jackpot with you, and I swear I'm going punch the next person who tries to tell me any different."

She gathered up her purse, "Now are you going to make me drive the rental illegally or are you coming with me?"

Nathan looked at her for a long, annoyed second. Then he set down his scotch and grabbed his keys. "Okay, let's go."

"Are you kidding me?" Andrew asked him. "You're the one who kept saying she was a psycho."

"She is a psycho, which is why I'm not about to let my crazy wife go after her alone. Are you coming or what?"

Before Andrew could answer, a sharp knock sounded on the door. "Hold on, I'm going to send whoever it is at the door away, then I'm going to come back and convince you and the real Layla why you have no business going after the woman who duped all of us."

But Andrew never did get to make that argument, because when he answered the door, he found two men in black suits standing on his porch.

"NYPD," said one of them, holding up a badge. "We're here to collect Roxxy RoxX. Though I think you might know her by her cover name." He stopped to check a piece of paper in his hand, then said. "I believe it's Layla."

"HERE, DRINK THIS," Roxxy's mother said on the way out of town. Shirelle jiggled a water bottle at her daughter, who was sitting in the passenger seat of the BMW with her arms folded. "It will make you feel better."

"Why, so you can drug me into submission?" Roxxy asked. "Just like you kept me doped up after you let that nasty man rape me?"

Her mother rolled her eyes. "Stop being so dramatic. You got a career most people can only dream of. I wish you'd just get over that already. Do you know what all I did to get you where you are now? It makes that incident you keep going on and on about feel like a walk in the park."

"I never asked you to do any of that stuff for me. I would have been satisfied just growing up like a normal kid, especially if I'd known I had a twin sister."

Shirelle glared at the road ahead. "I know you would have. You have it all, looks, dancing talent, and a great voice. And you never appreciated any of it. Or me. I'm the one who left your good-for-nothing father and your talentless sister behind. I'm the one who made everything happen for you. If I'd let you decide your own career path, you'd be some nobody living in Pittsburgh. Just like your sister."

"Layla isn't a nobody. She's my sister and one of the best people I've ever met."

The tires screeched, and Shirelle came to an abrupt stop at the side of the road. She turned to Roxxy with the crazed fervor of a zealot.

"She's a *nobody*, and the only reason anyone pays any attention to her is because she's married to a somebody." Shirelle nearly spat out the words. "I laid the world out at your feet. Millions of adoring fans, millions of records sold, and all you did was bitch and moan the entire time to the point that I had to keep you altered just to bear being in the same room with your ungrateful ass. Then I find out you're taking college classes behind my back and you were planning to start at USC this fall."

Roxxy's eyes narrowed. "How did you know that?"

"Oh please, Roxxy. I handle all your money, which includes paying your credit card bills. What did you think, you could just charge a semester at USC on your black American Express card without me noticing? Mabel, Dexter, that assistant D.A.—it's all your fault. If you had just kept on doing what I asked you to, nobody would have had to die or go to jail."

Realization began to sink in. "Oh, my God," Roxxy said. "It was you who killed Mabel and you who poisoned the tea Steve Kass drank. You switched it out when you came to visit me at the station before I left. And that's why the D.A. said Dexter's apartment looked like a movie cliché. You broke in while he was on vacation and planted all the evidence. But why? You can't possibly think I'm going to keep on singing after what you did."

"No, the plan was never for you to keep on singing. The plan was for you to die, supposedly at Dexter's hand. But as it turned out you were just Roxxy RoxX's assistant, a kind woman who looked like me and who also volunteered to pretend to be me and go into hiding so I wouldn't have to. The real Roxxy RoxX was going to be so overcome with grief, she'd vow to never sing again and would start acting. No makeup required."

That plan was so convoluted, it took Roxxy a few

puzzled moments to fully piece together what Shirelle was trying to tell her. "So you weren't just planning to murder me, but also to kill or incriminate everyone that's seen me without makeup and then take my place?"

"And maybe it would have stopped there, but you had to go and involve your sister, and those two other twins. Now I'm going to have to go back and take care of them after I get rid of you."

Her mother pulled a large, menacing needle out of her purse. "Why must you always make me do things the hard way?"

"No!" Roxxy said, turning to let herself out of the car. But it was too late. She felt the sharp prick of the needle in her back and she lost consciousness, thinking that this time her mother had literally stabbed her in the back.

CHAPTER 26

THERE were two roads leading out of town but the men from New York only had one car.

"We'll have to call the local police force for back up," said one of them.

"No, she has a half hour on us," Andrew answered. "That will take too long. You take the highway going toward Missoula, and I'll take the one going toward Buellton."

"We can't send a civilian after a possible kidnapper."

"Well, I'm going whether you like it or not. If you want, you can call the Buellton police department, too, but I'm going now."

"I'm coming with you," Nathan said, following him out the door.

"And me," Layla said.

They all jumped into his Chevy and peeled out without another word to the two men who'd come to get Roxxy, just a half hour too late.

It felt like a nightmare come true when they found the BMW by the side of the road. Andrew slammed on the brakes and was getting out the car, even before he finished turning over the ignition. But the rush was in vain.

"It's empty," he said to Nathan, who was close behind him. He looked around and pointed at the ground. "Look how this grass is depressed. It's like somebody was dragging something heavy through it."

"Or somebody," Layla said, looking toward the copse of trees in the distance.

ROXXY WOKE UP TO THE SOUND of metal scraping

against dirt. When she opened her eyes, the picture was blurry, but a few things were clear: she was now trussed up like a pig, with her wrists and ankles bound in thick rope.

And her mother was digging a grave.

"Good, you're awake," Shirelle said, when she saw Roxxy's eyes were open. "I was afraid you'd sleep through all of this."

"HELP!" Roxxy screamed. "Somebody please help!"

"Don't bother," Shirelle said. "We're about a mile from the road and in the middle of nowhere. Nobody can hear you."

As much as Roxxy had grown to love the wide, open spaces of Montana, she cursed them now, knowing her mother was right.

"You're not going to get away with this," she said to her mother.

"I think I've dug enough." Shirelle stuck the shovel in the ground. "They say you're supposed to make it six feet deep, but I don't think it really matters if you're not near a body of water. Three feet will do well enough."

Roxxy managed to get up on her feet despite her hands and ankles being tied together. "Somebody will figure it out. You can't just kill a rock star and two rich white guys without any investigation. They'll see through you, just like I'm seeing through you right now."

Roxxy must have hit a nerve, because Shirelle pulled a silver revolver on her. "Shut up," she said. "Just shut up."

Roxxy's eyes widened. "Where did you get a gun from? You can't fly with one of those."

Shirelle smiled, actual pride in her eyes. "No, but the wilderness store I got the rope and flashlight from sells them, and the man behind the counter was nice enough to let me buy one without a license. Unlike you, I've never had a problem using what I have to get what I want."

Roxxy gave her a disparaging look. "If what you had was that great, then you would have gotten the gun for free, not just a pass on the license. Think about this, Shirelle. You want to believe what I do is easy, but it's harder than it looks. It takes years of training and you've never even taken one acting class. People are going to have a hard time believing your story."

Her mother's sharp laugh rang out across the night sky. "That's what you want to believe, that you're oh-so-special, that you couldn't possibly be replaced. But your sister believed every word I said. So did her husband and her brother-in-law, who I assume you were sleeping with. So really, what *you* have isn't good enough."

Thinking of Andrew made Roxxy's heart burn with regret. As angry as she'd been when she walked out of the barn, she still loved him. And now she'd never get a chance to show him who she really was. And if her mother hurt him…her eyes filled with tears. Andrew and Layla had already been through so much. She hated that she had brought even more drama and violence into their lives.

"Please," she said. "Shoot me. But leave Layla and her family alone. They're good people, and they don't deserve to die."

"Nobody deserves anything. I sat by for years, watching you in the spotlight, knowing it should have been me. It would have been me if I'd had a mother who pushed me, if I hadn't gotten knocked up so young, and if I'd grown up during the era of auto tune."

Roxxy twisted her face. "That's a lot of conditions that would have had to be met in order for you to become famous, too."

"Shut up, you spoiled brat! I'm so sick of putting up with your constant whining and back talk. You're lucky I didn't kill you before now."

"No, I'm not lucky," Roxxy yelled back at her. "I think this entire situation pretty much highlights just how unlucky my entire life has been, and all because I was born to you, you selfish bitch!"

Shirelle's face curled into an ugly sneer and for a moment she actually looked her age. Forty-nine angry years written across her face.

A shot rang out, and Roxxy felt something hot pass into her chest. She coughed with the surprise of it all, and then pitched face forward into the fresh grave. But as she fell, she could have sworn she heard somebody scream. Layla?

ANDREW GRABBED THE REGISTERED GUN from his glove compartment, before taking off after Roxxy. He had never run so fast in his life, but Layla ran even faster. He distantly remembered her telling him she'd run track in high school when they'd been dating, and she obviously still had a talent for speed, because she shot past both him and Nathan and disappeared into the trees ahead of them.

Then the gunshot rang out.

"No!" they heard her scream a few moments later.

And just when Andrew thought he was at top speed, he found himself running even faster.

When he entered the trees, he found Layla trying to wrestle the gun out of Shirelle's hands.

His brain exploded with remembered pain. It was almost as if he'd come upon Layla and his dead wife wrestling for the gun again. But Shirelle must have been much stronger than Diana, because she soon gained the upper hand over Layla.

"If I had known you'd be such a problem, I would have

smothered you with a pillow before I left your no-good father."

She placed a hand at Layla's throat, choking her and raising the gun to shoot.

Andrew didn't think, he just raised his own gun and shot—once, twice, three times until Shirelle fell sideways and off of Layla, as dead as she'd been trying to make her daughter.

Nathan rushed past him, calling Layla's name and gathering her up in his arms. "Are you okay?" his brother asked, feeling all over his wife's body for possible injuries. "What is it with you and going after crazy women with guns in their hands?"

"I'm fine, thanks to Andrew," she answered. "But Roxxy…"

"Where is she?" Andrew looked around, but didn't see any sign of her. Then before Layla could answer, his stomach dropped. "No," he said when he saw the rectangle-shaped hole in the ground.

But his worse fear was confirmed when he came to stand over the grave and found Roxxy inside, blood splattered across the front of her white t-shirt.

ROXXY HAD BEEN ALL SET to die. The pain had finally started to fade away and a peaceful calm had stolen over her. But then she heard a voice calling her name. Her real name.

"Roxxy, Roxxy, no! Wake up, sweetheart." She felt herself being pulled out of the shallow grave.

It was Andrew, she realized, and he sounded so heartbroken that she couldn't help but do as he commanded.

"You're still alive," he said, when he came into view.

"Stay that way. We're going to get you to a hospital."

She grabbed his hand and managed to croak, "Andrew, the camp should be year round, and not just for underprivileged kids, but ones with developmental disabilities, too."

"Roxxy?" Layla came into view on the other side of Andrew, and she felt her twin grab her other hand.

Roxxy gave her a weak smile. "I'm glad I met you. I'm glad you're my sister."

Layla's eyes were teary with worry. "Please, just hold on. I can hear sirens in the distance. Help will be here soon."

It hurt to talk, but she had to tell Andrew one last thing. "My will still has Dexter as my main beneficiary. Just make sure he knows this is what I wanted and he'll give you the money for the camp."

"No, I'm not doing a damn thing for those kids without you," Andrew Sinclair, a man known throughout Montana for his charitable giving, answered. "If you want to change their lives through camp, then you better hang on, because I swear, I will kill the program if you die."

She shook her head. "Layla wouldn't let you do that."

"Oh yes, I would," Layla said. "Forget the children. I want my sister."

Roxxy would have laughed, except it hurt too much. "That's mean."

"I don't care," he said. "I need you to live."

And to her great surprise, he pulled a diamond ring out of nowhere and slipped it onto her finger. "I want you to be in my life forever."

"Even though I wasn't honest with you?" she asked.

"Fuck honesty," he said. "It's overrated. I just want to be with you. I don't care who you are."

Roxxy gave him a wobbly smile as tears filled her

eyes. It was exactly what he'd said in the dream, the one she'd woken up from this morning, knowing it couldn't possibly come true.

And even though there was a bright light in the far distance of her mind, practically calling her name, she decided then and there to hold on tight to Andrew, to hold on tight to life.

After all she'd put Andrew through, she figured it was the least she could do.

EPILOGUE

New Year's Day

UNLIKE when Roxxy had come to the Sinclair Chalet the first time, the ski lodge was at full capacity on her wedding day. Over three hundred guests had shown up for the formal ceremony and reception despite the remote location and the holiday date. And the scene inside was the very picture of glamorous elegance.

Elegant save for the twin sisters in the bathroom of the lodge's largest honeymoon suite, that is.

"You know, this is kind of gross, right?" Roxxy said to her sister as she gingerly handled the clear plastic cup, which was filled to the halfway point with her own urine. She held it as far away from her body as possible, so as not to spill a drop of it on her couture wedding dress, even though holding her arm in such a position exacerbated the wound on her chest. It had been over six months since she'd gotten shot, and Layla had guided her through her physical therapy beautifully, but it still ached a little when she held out her arm for too long.

Roxxy didn't mind. She considered it a small price to pay for gaining the kind of happiness she could have never imagined, even in her best dreams.

Layla was also wearing a fancy dress of her own, a floor-length, dark green matron of honor gown to be exact. But she seemed much more sure-handed with her own half-full cup of urine. "I'm in the medical profession. It takes a lot to gross me out. Plus, I'm too excited to feel anything but happy right now."

Roxxy hesitated with the pregnancy test stick hovering

above her cup in the air. "Maybe we should wait until tomorrow. That way you can drink champagne during the toast."

"I've already set aside a bottle of sparkling cider for the table. If it turns out either of us is pregnant, we can both drink it in solidarity. If not, then no worries if I do."

Roxxy smiled fondly at her sister. When they'd finally been able to get their hands on Roxxy's birth certificate, they'd discovered that Layla had been born first. It had only been three minutes, but at times like this, Roxxy definitely felt like the younger sister.

"Okay," she said, taking a deep breath. "Let's do it."

Five minutes later they checked the results and screamed in unison.

Perhaps not the wisest move, considering that Dexter came crashing through the bathroom door just a few seconds later.

"It's okay, Dex," Roxxy told him just as he drew his gun, eyes scanning the room for somebody to shoot. "We just found out we're both pregnant. We screamed because we were happy, not because we were in danger."

Dexter re-sheathed his gun in its side holster with a big grin on his face. If he was harboring even an ounce of resentment about the two nights he'd spent in jail because of their mother's scheming, you couldn't tell it at that moment. Not only had he made a special trip to give Roxxy away at her wedding, he'd also been handling security for the chalets, which was now swarming with press outside, despite the cold mountain temperatures. The story of how Roxxy RoxX had come to discover her long lost twin sister, fall in love with her brother-in-law, and get shot by her own mother, had made national headlines, and photogs were practically chomping at the bit to get pics of the wedding that would cap it all.

But at that moment, the circus outside became Dex's last concern. He placed a large hand over Roxxy's belly and asked, "Do you think you'll have twins, too?"

"Not likely," Layla answered, her voice apologetic. "Usually it skips a generation. But we might have twin grandbabies to look forward to."

Imagining that made Roxxy and Layla scream anew.

But then they heard the sound of footsteps running into the suite.

"Layla!" Nathan called, at the same time Andrew called out, "Roxxy?"

They appeared in their groom and best man's tuxes in the doorway with identical looks of fear and confusion on their identical faces.

This time Layla really did scream. "Get out, Andrew," she commanded. "Don't you know it's bad luck to see the bride before the wedding?"

Neither Andrew nor Nathan budged.

"The last time we heard you scream, your mother had shot your sister, so you'll understand why we came running," Nathan said.

Layla giggled. "Don't be silly. I'm fine. We were screaming because we're pregnant!"

Their eyes went wide and they said, "Both of you?" at the same time.

"Both of us," Layla and Roxxy answered back in stereo.

Nathan yelled, "Yes!" and scooped Layla into his arms. But Andrew just stayed where he was, his gray eyes burning hot into Roxxy's.

"Andrew?" she asked tentatively. When she had been admitted to the hospital, she'd also gone ahead and had her IUD taken out since it had been five years. But in her six months of recovery, she and Andrew hadn't really discussed the possibility of children, or whether he even wanted them.

"Get out," he said. "Everybody but Roxxy, get out right now."

"It really is bad luck to see the bride before the wedding," Layla started.

"Nathan, unless you want me to physically remove your wife from this suite myself, I suggest you get her out of here," Andrew answered.

With a few insistent words from Dexter and a few more good-natured grumbles from Layla they all cleared out, leaving Roxxy and her fiancé alone.

For a moment, Roxxy was afraid she'd made a terrible mistake. Maybe Andrew didn't want kids and had thought she'd gone on the pill when she got the IUD taken out.

But then he crossed the room and kissed her, holding her so close, she could feel the joy vibrating throughout his body, and another part of him hard against her stomach.

"So I take it you're happy about the news."

Andrew shook his head at her, "Yesterday, I was just thinking I'd never been happier. But today, you've just made me the happiest man on earth. I'm so fucking glad you came into my life."

Roxxy smiled. "Language, language, Mr. Sinclair. Is that how you talk to the mother of your future children? That's not very gentlemanly of you."

She started to undo his pants, and Andrew smiled, obviously liking where she was going with this.

"You see that's just it, Roxxy. I thought I was a gentleman before I met you. Nathan was supposed to be the bad boy twin. But I guess in the end, I'm really the wild one."

Roxxy grinned. "Good, because as it turns out, I'm the wild one, too."

Then they showed each other just how wild they were up against the bathroom door.

The two people, who had thought themselves unlucky before meeting each other, didn't worry at all about bad luck that day. The universe had conspired to bring them together through the most unlikely set of circumstances either of them could have ever imagined. And now they had one another, the baby growing inside of Roxxy, and a passion for each other that felt like it would never fade.

No, of this one thing they were certain. They were definitely the luckiest people on earth.

If you liked this story, check out the other books in the 50 Loving State series:

THE OWNER OF HIS HEART
HER RUSSIAN BILLIONAIRE
HER VIKING WOLF

Theodora Taylor reads, writes, and reviews in Pittsburgh, Pennsylvania. When not reading, writing, or reviewing, she enjoys going to the movies, daydreaming, and attending dinner parties thrown by others with her wonderful husband. Feel free to contact her at theodorawrites@gmail.com, and if you love IR romance as much as she does, check out her review blog at irbookreviews.com

Printed in Great Britain
by Amazon.co.uk, Ltd.,
Marston Gate.